JOE HOWE
TO THE RESCUE

Joe Howe
to the *Rescue*

Michael Bawtree

Illustrations by
David Preston Smith

NIMBUS
PUBLISHING LTD

Nimbus Publishing Limited
PO Box 9166
Halifax, NS   B3K 5M8
(902) 455-4286

Cover and interior illustrations: David Preston Smith
Cover and interior design: Kathy Kaulbach, Paragon Design Group
Author photo: Wendy Elliott

Printed and bound in Canada

Library and Archives Canada Cataloguing in Publication

Bawtree, Michael
Joe Howe to the rescue / Michael Bawtree ;
illustrations by David Preston Smith.
ISBN 1-55109-495-9
1. Howe, Joseph, 1804-1873—Juvenile fiction. 2. Halifax (N.S.)—History—19th century—Juvenile fiction. I. Smith, David Preston II. Title.

PS8553.A85J64 2004   jC813'.54   C2004-904028-6

We acknowledge the financial support of the Government of Canada through the Book Publishing Industry Development Program (BPIDP) and the Canada Council for our publishing activities.

CONTENTS

CHAPTER ONE

JOE HOWE TO THE RESCUE

A long time ago, when the crooked streets in the old port town of Halifax were full of horses and carts, and rich carriages, and tinkers, and fiddlers, and companies of soldiers, and beautiful women in long dresses, a boy named Jack lived with his mother, Mrs. Dance, in a run-down little wooden house at the north end of town.

Jack's father, Henry Dance, was the captain of a merchant ship, but he had sailed away on the *Mary Lou* over a year ago, and neither Jack nor his mother had heard a word of him since. Mrs. Dance was sure he had drowned somewhere out in the ocean. But she never told her son about these fears, and almost every day after school Jack would run down to the docks and gaze out past McNab's Island, past the lighthouse, toward the open sea. Perhaps today was the day *Mary Lou* would come dipping into port, its rusty brown sails crowding, and its prow cutting through the swell. "Father!" he found himself crying out, imagining the familiar figure striding towards him. And he would run and jump into his father's arms.

No sign of the *Mary Lou* today. No sign of Captain Dance. Jack sighed. He turned away and wandered through the bustling wharves. Dock workers were unloading big crates of sugar and tubs of molasses from the Caribbean, and bales of cloth from Liverpool, and fish from the cold waters here in Nova Scotia. A group of sailors passed him shouting and singing. An old man was roasting chestnuts over a brazier and offering them to the passers-by. Peddlers were selling trinkets: silver bracelets from Peru, brooches of ivory, wooden animals. Christmas was not far away, and Jack would have liked to buy something for his mother, but he had not a penny in his pocket. And anyway he knew his mother would scold him if he brought her a present. "We can't afford such things, you silly boy," she would say. He took a last look down the harbour, and turned sadly for home.

They were poor. Very poor. Captain Dance had managed to buy their small house, and he had set aside enough money to send Jack to a small school in the north of the town. But he had been gone for many long months, and the funds he had put by for his son's education had finally run out. Mrs. Dance had found a job caring for the children of one of the magistrates who ran the affairs of the town, but it was sometimes weeks at a time before she got paid, and the pay was miserable. The magistrate and his wife were rude and snooty to her, and every day she was glad when she could close the big door behind her and tramp back to her little house. How much longer can I go on like this, she thought. She had been trying to keep Jack at school for a time, but she could no longer afford the pennies it cost her. Jack was going to have to go out to work soon, and be done with this school nonsense. She let herself in, took off her bonnet, and put on some potatoes for supper.

❧

"Get out of my way, you scamp!" snarled a big, burly carter, stepping heavily back from his cart with a barrel over his shoulder, and nearly knocking Jack off the wooden sidewalk into the street. Jack picked himself up and looked angrily back at the big man.

"Look where you're going, why don't you!" he cried.

"Don't you talk back to me!" shouted the man furiously. He put down his barrel and lunged at Jack. Jack skipped out of his way, but found himself held by another man, a tall, skinny young fellow with a red nose and a silly smile on his face.

"Here he be, Ezra," said the skinny fellow: "Wanna teach him a lesson?"

"Sure I do," growled Ezra, lunging at poor Jack, who struggled in vain to get free.

"I wouldn't do that if I were you," said a voice. It was quiet, but it was firm, and Ezra looked up to see a smartly dressed man wearing a tall hat and a grey coat. He was carrying a stout cane, and looked as though he wouldn't put up with any nonsense.

"Oh, gooday to yer, Mr. Howe…we was just havin' a little fun, wasn't we, b'y?"

The skinny man let go of Jack and smiled stupidly.

"Jus' some fun, tha's all," he said.

"Are you all right, lad?" asked Mr. Howe.

"Perfectly fine," said Jack, dusting himself off.

"Here, I'll walk you home a little way. You watch your step, Ezra, or you'll be back in the lock-up. You too, Silver," he added, turning to the skinny man.

"Yessir."

"Come along with me, lad."

Jack's rescuer put his arm round the boy's shoulders, and they climbed the steep, muddy street away from the port. Halifax was a garrison town then, with soldiers guarding the docks and the ships in the harbour, ready to defend the whole coast of Nova Scotia. Fort George stood on the high hill at the end of the street, its high new walls frowning fiercely down at the busy scene below.

"So what's your name?" asked Mr. Howe as they walked along. Jack almost had to skip to keep up with the swift stride of his new friend.

"Jack, sir – Jack Dance."

"That's a fine name. I'm Joseph Howe."

"You mean the Mr. Howe that owns *The Novascotian*?"

"Yes, that's the one. Joe, they call me."

"Yes, sir. It's very good to meet you."

Jack knew the name well. So did most of the townspeople of

Halifax. *The Novascotian* newspaper was famous for speaking up for the people of Nova Scotia, and specially for caring about the poor and the mistreated. Joe Howe often upset the high-ups running the town by showing up their crooked ways, and Mrs. Dance, who always bought the paper no matter how poor she was, would chuckle with delight as she read Jack the latest fire-cracker from Joe's pen. Jack was not too interested at first, but he got to look forward to these weekly sessions with his mother, and was beginning to know quite a lot about the rotten things that were going on. And now there was Joe Howe walking beside him and saluting people left and right. Almost everyone knew Joe. Jack felt very important.

"Now where do you live, Jack?"

"Just off Gottingen Street, sir. William Alley."

"I am always ready for a stroll," said Mr. Howe. "I'll take you there."

"You don't have to do that, sir. I go all over town on my own."

"Oh, I can see you look after yourself. But I like company. Don't you?"

"Surely I do, sir. Thank you very much."

The pair of them turned up Jacob Street heading towards the north end of the town. Jack was quiet at first, but Mr. Howe was so entertaining, so interesting, that soon he had Jack laughing and chatting away as if they had been friends for years.

"Did you know those men who were going to hit me?" asked Jack.

"Certainly I did. They work for Mr. Hemple, one of the mag-istrates who run this old town. And they're up to no good. You saw those barrels?"

"I sure did."

"I'm pretty sure they are full of rum, being smuggled from Jamaica."

"Is that why you were there?"

"Yes, I'm writing something about their business—for my paper."

"You wrote something about Mr. Hemple last week too,

didn't you?"

They were turning up Gottingen Street. Joe Howe stopped dead in his tracks and turned to the boy in amazement.

"You mean you read *The Novascotian*?"

"Oh yes. Well, my mother reads it out to me, and sometimes I read it for myself."

"Well I'm blessed! How old are you?"

"I've just turned twelve."

"Do you attend school?"

"Yes I go to Mrs. Pringle's on Brunswick Street. But I'm finishing soon. My father's been away at sea for over a year, and Mum can't afford to send me any more."

Joe Howe frowned and shook his head but said nothing. They continued their walk, and were soon at Jack's home. Joe put out his hand, and the boy shook it eagerly.

"Well, goodbye for now, Jack. I'll be seeing you again, I reckon."

"I hope so, sir. And thank you for getting me away from those bullies."

"Glad I did. I picked up a new friend. Now you look after yourself."

Jack watched as Joe Howe strode rapidly off down the alley and out of sight. Then he ran in excitedly to his mother.

"Mum, Mum! Guess who I met!"

"Oh I wouldn't know. Look, supper's on the table. Come and sit down."

"Mum! I met Mr. Howe! – Joe Howe!"

Mrs. Dance looked at him.

"You're jesting."

"No – I promise!"

And as they sat down to eat, Jack told her the story of how he had nearly been beaten, and how Mr. Howe rescued him, and how they talked and talked as he walked Jack home. Mrs. Dance pretended not to take much interest, but really she was glowing with pride. Joe Howe was her hero. And to think her son had shaken his hand!

Jack soon finished his meal. It was already dark, for this was late November and the days were drawing in. He did some homework in the kitchen where it was warm, while his mother sat by the stove knitting him a pair of socks. But he couldn't keep his mind on what he was doing. He kissed his mother goodnight, took his candle and went off to bed. His room wasn't much bigger than a clothes closet, but it was his and he loved it. He blew out the candle, and tossed and turned in bed for a while. But soon he was fast asleep.

CHAPTER TWO

JACK GETS A LETTER

J ack was small for his age, with brown hair and startling grey eyes. He was thin and wiry, but he had strong hands and moved with quick, darting steps. People used to say that he stood out of the crowd in spite of his size, and that he was "goin' somewheres." He was known at Mrs. Pringle's as a boy who would always stick up for the small ones. He hated to see bullies throwing their weight about in the little playground behind the school, and often rushed in to protect them. He had a temper too, and even the bigger boys were just a little bit afraid of him.

Next morning he was up early and out of the house, with his satchel over his back, for the twenty-minute walk to school. His mother had told him that when Christmas came he would have to leave, and he was sad as he walked through the old gates of Mrs. Pringle's house. He greeted his friends. Tim Overton came up to try and sell him a bright green glass marble that he had found in the street the day before. Sam wanted some help with the French exercises they had been given. Dick asked him to a party planned for the weekend. Everyone was talking and chatting as the school bell rang and they all trooped in to class.

As Jack went down the corridor to his classroom, a heavy-set boy stood in his way. Jack stopped and looked up at him. He tried to pass but the boy wouldn't let him by.

"What on earth − ?" asked Jack.

"Toadying up with that no-good Joe Howe, are you, little Jackyboy?"

It was Harry…what was his last name? Jack tried to remember. Harry…Hemple – yes, that's it. Just a minute – he remembered the men loading the barrels down by the dock, and Joe Howe saying something about Mr. Hemple the magistrate. And he remembered reading about him too, something about shady dealings at the town office. This Harry must be Mr. Hemple's son.

"Joe Howe's my friend," said Jack.

"Oh, is he?" Harry Hemple stood over him menacingly.

"You won't scare me," said Jack, giving Harry a big shove and walking past him into class.

"I'll get you," snarled Harry after him as he turned off into another classroom. Jack didn't reply.

When school was over for the day Jack said goodbye to his friends and started out for home. In the light breeze from the harbour the trees were losing their last dead leaves, which crackled underfoot as he walked along. He thought about Harry Hemple. Harry must have seen him with Joe Howe the day before. But why was he so threatening? Mr. Howe must have enemies. With all the things he said in *The Novascotian*, perhaps that was not surprising. And now he remembered that his mother had heard her master and mistress talking about Joe Howe as though he should be locked up. His new friend could be in danger, Jack thought.

As he lifted the latch of the back door, his mother called out to him.

"Is that you, Jack?"

"Yes, Mum. How was work today?" He loved his mother dearly, and hated the thought of her looking after other people's children

"There's a letter for you. Come open it."

"A letter?" thought Jack. He couldn't remember ever getting a letter from anyone – except years ago from his dad. And that wasn't really a letter at all, because Henry Dance could never be bothered with putting words to paper. Instead, he had sent his son pages and pages of pictures he had drawn, as he went from port to port in South America. Jack had treasured these, and some of them were still pinned up on the wall of his room. Was this another crop of drawings like those?

"Where's it from?"

"Here in Halifax. Someone left it in the door." She handed him an envelope, and on it he read his name, "Mr. Jack Dance," in a strong, flowing hand. He cut open the envelope with a knife, and took out a single sheet of paper. He held it to the light of the candle and read:

Dear Jack,

I was happy to meet you the other day. In our chat you told me you would soon be leaving your school and looking for a position. You're very young to be working, and I don't like the thought of you having to finish school so early because of lack of funds: no one should have to pay for their schooling. But then I had an idea: would you like to come and work for me at The Novascotian? We could do with an office boy to keep things tidy, run messages, and help about the place, and I think you might be just the right lad for the job. When you are a little older perhaps you can become an apprentice in my printshop.

Talk it over with your mother, and if she approves come and see me next Monday after school.

Your friend,
Joe Howe

Silently, but with shining eyes, Jack handed the letter to his mother. She wiped her hands on her apron, took the letter and read it. She read it again. Then she burst into tears. Jack went over and hugged her tight.

"Don't you want me to do it?" he asked.

"Oh yes. Yes, yes. I'm crying because I'm so happy. Dear Jack." And she kissed him on the top of his head.

That same evening, with his mother's help, he wrote a reply to Joe Howe:

Dear Mr. Howe,
Thank you for your letter. I was happy to know that there might be
a chance to work for you at your newspaper. I will come to your office
at five o'clock in the afternoon on Monday, as you suggested.
Respectfully,
Jack Dance

He folded the letter in two, and – using the flame of the candle to melt some wax – sealed it tight. Very early next morning, while it was still dark, he ran all the way to Granville Street. The office of *The Novascotian* was almost opposite the great pile of building called Province House, where the King's Council and the Assembly did the business of the country. He dropped his letter in the office mailbox and then ran all the way back, arriving at Mrs. Pringle's just in time for the first class. He was bursting to tell his news to his friends Tim and Sam and Dick, but managed to keep quiet. What if he didn't get the job? Then he would look really silly. Besides, that nasty Harry Hemple might hear of it, and who knows what that might lead to?

∽

The following Monday, Jack arrived at *The Novascotian* just as the garrison clock struck five. Joe Howe was sitting in his small office inside the door, in his shirtsleeves, with a large quill pen in his hand.

"Jack, good to see you. Now you just sit there a moment, will you, while I finish off this article for the printers – I'm late as usual and I mustn't miss tomorrow's paper."

Joe went back to his writing, scratching the words with furious speed. Jack sat on the edge of a big wooden armchair and looked around him. Joe's large oak desk was so covered with books and papers and documents that you couldn't see the top of it at all. A map of Nova Scotia hung above the mantle of a slate fireplace, where a coal fire was singing away. On the mantle was a silhouette picture of an old-looking man, and another of a pretty young woman. In the corner was the plaster bust of a bald man with a beard. Jack got up to take a close look, and read the name on the base of the bust: W. SHAKSPEAR. So that's what he looked like, Jack thought.

"Ever read any Shakespeare?" asked Joe, who had finished his writing and was collecting his papers.

"Mrs. Pringle sometimes reads bits of it to us, but we don't really understand it."

"Ah, that's because she probably doesn't understand it herself. We'll have to look at him together one day."

"Do you have time to read that stuff?" asked Jack wonderingly.

"It's my food," replied Joe with a smile. He hit a small bell. A young apprentice ran in from the print-shop behind the office. He had tousled red hair, and his hands were stained with ink.

"Here you are, my boy – take these to Mr. McNab. By the way, this is young Mr. Dance. He may be coming to work with us here as printer's devil. Jack, this is Rob Woollings."

The boys nodded, and Rob ran back into the shop with Joe's sheets of paper. Jack looked puzzled.

"Printer's devil, sir?"

"Ah, yes – don't be alarmed! That's what printers call their office boy. So you might be interested in joining us here at *The Novascotian*, eh?"

"Yes, sir."

"Well then, come and take a look around and meet my staff."

Joe put on his coat, and dived into the print-shop followed by Jack, wide-eyed and excited beyond belief. For the next hour they scrambled around printing presses, saw type being set line by line in lead trays, smelt the pungent printer's ink, toured the store room with its stacks of paper, and met a whole lot of people, from Mr. McNab, who was Joe Howe's head printer and managed the shop, to the typesetters and the other apprentices. As the tour came to an end, there was a clacking and a thumping sound from the middle of the room, and Jack turned round just in time to see an apprentice cranking a large handle, and another lifting the first sheet of the latest *Novascotian* off the press.

"So – what do you think, Jack?" asked Joe.

"I'll start tomorrow if you want, sir."

"No, you finish school and start with us right after Christmas. A printer's devil works eight to five, with Sundays off. Five shillings a week to begin with: is that fair?" Joe Howe looked Jack straight in the eye, with a faint smile on his lips.

"Quite fair, sir."

"Good man!"

They shook hands, to seal the bargain. Jack put on his cap and his threadbare jacket, hurriedly said goodbye, and raced home to tell his mother the news. He was happier than he had ever been in his life.

CHAPTER THREE

GOODBYE, MRS. PRINGLE

The three weeks left before the holiday passed so slowly Jack thought they would never end. But fall turned slowly to winter, and finally the blustery day when school broke up for Christmas arrived. News of his job had got around to the teachers, and old Mrs. Pringle, who disapproved of Joe Howe, called Jack into her drawing-room and gave him a stern warning.

"Take the position, young man. You'll do well – you're a bright lad. But don't you go down Mr. Howe's road, whatever you do. He makes trouble for God-fearing people like our councillors and magistrates, who work so hard for us. He even writes rudely about our governor! Respect, Mr. Dance. He has no respect. Don't go down his road."

"I'll keep my eyes open, Mrs. Pringle," replied Jack, "but I have to say I think Mr. Howe has some good ideas, and I hope to learn from him. He knows all about Shakespeare too."

Mrs. Pringle's eyes narrowed. The small boy standing in front of her holding his cap looked innocent enough, but was he suggesting he would be learning more from Mr. Howe than he had learnt from her? She wasn't sure. The pleats of her long black silk dress swirled and rustled as she turned away angrily to her desk, and the dark red garnets of her necklace clattered together.

"Here's your last report. Take it to your mother. And remember: respect, respect, respect!"

"Goodbye, Mrs. Pringle," said Jack cheerfully, taking the report but apparently taking no notice of her advice. He walked to the door, then turned back: "Oh, and – Merry Christmas, Mrs. P.!"

Mrs. Pringle pursed her lips and didn't reply. Jack closed the door behind him. He was free! He said goodbye to his friends and promised to go skating with them over the holiday, down on Billy's Pond, as soon as the ice was thick enough.

Outside the school gate Jack caught sight of Harry Hemple, who was being met by his father in a smart carriage drawn by two chestnut horses. Harry was climbing into the carriage, and as the door closed and the horses began moving away, they passed right by Jack. Harry looked down and saw his enemy and stuck his tongue out. Then Jack watched him lean over and say something to his father, who turned to catch a glimpse of the boy. Soon they were round the corner and out of sight.

It was starting to snow, and Jack hurried home through the darkening streets. Many of the stores were open late because Christmas was approaching. There was holly and mistletoe hanging at the shop doors, and lanterns and red candles lighting their windows. Groceries, bakers, shoe shops, toyshops—they all looked dazzling and made him want to buy something, anything. He still had a few pennies from shopping for his mother the day before, and he hesitated, jingling them in his pocket. But no, he would have to wait until he started earning. He sighed and turned into William Alley, his boots making a crunching sound in the freshly fallen snow.

As Jack came up to his front door he was surprised to find it open. He walked in calling out "Mother!" as he always did, and got another surprise. Their next door neighbour Mrs. Transom was rushing down the cramped little staircase with a washbasin full of water. "Oh Jack, there you are!" she said, putting down the basin and almost falling into a chair. Jack looked at her. Her grey hair had fallen over her kindly old face, and she was perspiring. She began wiping her brow with a cloth.

"What is it?" said Jack, his heart pounding. "Is something wrong?" He started towards the stairs.

"Just a minute now, boy. It's your mother. She collapsed outside in the street, on her way home from work. We think it might be…" she trailed off.

"Cholera?" said Jack at once. Mrs. Transom nodded. There had been a terrible epidemic of the disease in Halifax all that year. Many people had been sick, and some had died, including the whole family of one of his school friends. He rushed upstairs. His mother was lying in bed, propped up on pillows. She was pale as a lily, her hands clutching and unclutching. There was a sickening stench in the little room.

"Mummy!" He went towards her.

"Don't touch me, dear. You never know. I'll be all right." Jack found himself starting to cry, and he turned away. "I'll be back, Mum." He rushed back downstairs.

"We must get a doctor."

"Oh, doctors don't come much to this part of town – you know that," said Mrs. Transom getting up from her chair. "She needs plenty of water and that's what we've been giving her. I'm bringing some clean linen just as soon as I can get it from home. Jack, why don't you –?"

But she didn't finish what she was saying because Jack had snatched up his cap and dashed out through the door. She hurried outside, just in time to see him running helter-skelter through the heavily falling snow to the end of the alley and out of sight.

As usual, Joe Howe was working late at the newspaper. He heard a rapid knock at the door, and went to open it.

"Jack! What are you doing here?"

"It's my mother, sir. She's very sick and she needs a doctor. We think it might be the cholera."

Joe looked at the panting boy in front of him and immediately dropped his pen, jumped up, grabbed his long coat and his tall hat and said:

"Come with me."

Things happened so fast that afterwards Jack could hardly remember what happened when. One moment they were knocking at a door on Sackville Street. Next they were hurrying through the house, following a man in a black coat, still eating a chicken drumstick from his dinner. He picked up a black bag in the back hallway and went outside calling for his stable boy. Next moment they were gliding along Barrack Street below the Citadel in the doctor's sleigh, pulling rugs over themselves against the raw wind off the harbour. And then they were in William Alley, and bundling inside Mrs. Dance's little home. Mrs. Transom was still in the kitchen boiling up water, and was taken aback by the sudden arrival of two big men. The doctor sped up the stairs without even asking the way, calling out as he went: "Bring up that hot water!" and leaving Jack and Joe Howe below. Mrs. Transom hurried behind him with a kettle.

"You did the right thing, Jack," said Joe, settling into the chair by the stove. "With cholera you have to move fast. And Dr. Gregor knows more about it than anyone in town. Come on, let's brew up some tea. Can you do that?"

"Yes, of course, sir," said Jack. He filled a pot from the pump in the corner and put it on the stove. And all the time he was listening to the sounds from upstairs.

"Shall I go up, sir?"

"No, you leave them up there. They'll be down soon enough." He saw the stricken look on the boy's face, and knew he must somehow be distracted. He looked over to the table.

"Why, here's today's paper. Did you read it?"

"No sir. I haven't had time."

"Read this." He folded over the double sheet of *The Novascotian*, tapped on one of the columns and passed it to Jack, who took it over to the candle and began to read.

We are told by the magistrates who run our fair town that they have finally brought smuggling under control. This news will be well received by those of us who have been convinced that there is a lot going on down by the docks which seems to escape the eye of the authorities. It was just the other day that I saw what looked and smelt like barrels of rum being loaded into a certain warehouse by a couple of gentlemen I have known in less respectable circumstances. The only odd thing about it was that the barrels were labelled PITCH. If that was pitch I wouldn't waste it on our roofs! Let us hope their worships are going to keep up their patrols — and that none of them are involved in the business they claim to be closing down.

Jack looked over at Joe Howe.

"That was the day I met you!"

"That very day." He was going to say more, but there was noise on the stairs, and Dr. Gregor came down, bending low to avoid the beam overhead. He was drying his hands on a cloth, and his grey-bearded face was serious. Jack looked up at him.

"I think we got here just in time, young lad. But your mother is very, very weak and dehydrated. She is going to have to be moved to the infirmary where we can nurse her properly."

"But we could never afford that," exclaimed Jack. "She'll have to stay here. I can look after her."

The doctor and Joe Howe exchanged glances.

"We'll get her there first, Jack," said Joe quietly, "and then we'll sort it out. And you won't be staying here by yourself either. You'll come to my house until your mother's better. My wife will set you up a room in the attic soon enough."

And so it was that before the end of the evening Mrs. Dance was sleeping comfortably between linen sheets in Dr. Head's Infirmary on Lower Water Street. And her son Jack was lying in a small cot under the eaves in Joe Howe's sprawling home on Granville, only two doors down from the newspaper office. His adventures had well and truly begun.

CHAPTER FOUR

A CHRISTMAS VISITOR

I t was the day before Christmas Eve, and Mrs. Dance was finally on the mend. It had been an anxious time, and Jack had walked over to the infirmary every day from Joe Howe's home, to read to his mother, bring her fruit, and run errands for her. She was anxious to be back in her own house for Christmas, but Joe Howe wouldn't hear of it. He had come with Jack that day especially to give her an invitation, and was now sitting down beside the bed, grasping her hand with a smile.

"You're coming to spend Christmas with us, Mrs. Dance."

"Oh I couldn't, Mr. Howe, really I couldn't."

"Nonsense," said Joe vigorously. "I've talked to Mrs. Howe and we have a room all ready for you on the main floor, so you won't have to climb stairs until you're stronger. Besides, how can we spend Christmas without Jack? He's part of the family."

Mrs. Dance was soon persuaded, and Jack was thrilled beyond words. Each day for the past two weeks he had told his mother about his exciting life with the Howes since he had moved in. He had made fast friends with Mr. Howe's son, Edward, who was just seven but old for his age and full of mischief. He played with little Ellen, and even held the new baby Josey in his arms. Mr. Howe's father, kindly old Mr. John Howe, visited almost every day, and would often have a word with the young visitor. Jack was a single child himself, and this was the first time in his life he had found himself in the middle of a large, noisy family. He loved it. And every evening, when Joe Howe came home from the newspaper office, the fire would be stoked up in the big drawing room and they would all crowd round, talking and laughing. Sometimes Joe would read to them all, and then, after the young ones – including Edward – had been packed off to bed, Joe would sit and chat about serious matters with his wife Susan Ann – and also with Jack, who was allowed to stay up an hour longer.

This was the time he looked forward to most. Joe would give him a little mug of weak beer, and help himself to a glass of rum, which he would mix with water and sip slowly. Mrs. Howe would drink tea, and very often would be working on the accounts of the newspaper while they talked. Jack was used to his mother sewing or knitting, and he was amazed to see Susan Ann with her elegant sleeves rolled back, working away at ledgers and invoices – like a man, he thought. Jack was an observant boy; with his sharp eyes and ears he took in everything around him.

∞

"Susan Ann, dearest," Joe said one night, "I don't know what you are making of those figures, but we continue to be in some trouble, do we not? Things are so depressed at the moment all over Nova Scotia. Having a lot of subscribers is no use if they are not paying up. How am I going to keep on looking after you and the darlings?"

"You know what I say, Joe. Things will turn around – they always do. We just have to hold on, and pray a little."

Joe laughed.

"It's what I believe."

Jack loved Mrs. Howe. She had dark hair and a pretty, strong face, and moved around the house almost at a run, getting through her many tasks as housewife, mother to the three young children and Joe's business partner. They employed a cook, a woman from Preston named Hannah, and also a housemaid, whose name was Betty. But Susan Ann seemed to work harder than either of them, and still had time to make Jack as welcome in the house as her own son.

Jack spoke up.

"One problem, sir, is that you are too generous."

Joe and Susan Ann both looked round in surprise. They had almost forgotten the small figure in the corner, nursing his little mug of beer.

"Now look, Jack – " began Joe.

"No, I mean it, sir. You have been so kind to me and now you say my mother is joining us for Christmas. Everywhere I go they talk about how you lend people money, and have them for dinner if they are hard up. It seems to me you have to have a lot of money before you can do that kind of thing."

Joe and Susan Ann exchanged smiles. She had often told him just the same thing in almost the same words.

"Jack," answered Joe, "don't ever think that you can only be generous if you have money. In fact – "

"I don't mean to be ungrateful, sir, but I hate to see you and Mrs. Howe worrying. Mother and I can take care of ourselves."

"Look, Jack, it's Christmastime: if ever there was a time for giving a helping hand to people, it's now. And anyway, you won't be getting off so lightly, my lad. Once the new year starts, you're going to be a great help to me in the office. There are a lot of things going on in this town just at the moment, and I'll soon need all the friends I can get."

Jack looked up inquiringly at Joe's big, generous face.

"Oh, don't bother him with all that, dear. He's far too young to be troubled with Halifax politics."

"You'd be surprised, dear. Jack reads *The Novascotian* as carefully as people twice his age. Don't you, Jack?"

"I certainly do read it, sir. And, by the way, I know there are a lot of people who say you are playing with fire, the way you wrote about the magistrates last month. But I think you are right. It's terrible what's going on."

"Good for you, Jack!" laughed Joe, looking at his surprised wife, who had put down her pen in amazement.

"What do *you* know about what's going on?" asked Susan Ann.

"Well, here's one thing. Miss Hogg who lives at the end of our street had her house pulled down by the town a few years ago so as to stop a fire spreading. And she still hasn't been paid for it. She's been in real trouble. They owe her more than a hundred pounds. And then the other day they nearly arrested her because she owed them a couple of pounds in taxes."

"Yes, I've heard of similar cases," said Joe, pulling a pencil out of his pocket and making a note. "See here, Jack: you keep your ear to the ground, and if you hear other stories like that you let me know, will you? Now, it's past your bedtime. Give Mrs. Howe a kiss, and off you go."

"Yes, sir." Jack went upstairs, and to bed. His mind was whirling, but he was soon asleep, dreaming of adventure.

Mrs. Dance was brought to the house in the doctor's own sleigh on Christmas Eve. It had snowed hard again that morning, and the whole town was covered in white and looked prettier than anyone had ever seen it. Betty and Hannah helped the invalid to her room, where she was soon tucked up in bed and made to feel as comfortable as could be. Jack was allowed to bring young Edward and Ellen to say hello, but they could only come just inside the door, for fear of Mrs. Dance's recent illness. Old Mr. Howe also came in, and prayed with her for a few minutes. Jack was thrilled and proud to have his mother with him in what had almost become his new home.

He was just blowing out her candle when they both heard a loud knocking at the front door. Jack often liked to beat Betty to the door and now he ran out crying, "Goodnight, mother!" over his shoulder, and raced to the front of the house. He grabbed hold of the big brass doorknob and pulled the heavy door open. On the steps, sheltering from the snow, stood a man dressed in a long topcoat, scarf, gloves and boots, and wearing a tall brown hat. He was carrying a slim leather case. Jack had never seen him before, but he looked very distinguished. Jack said, "Good evening, sir," just as Joe came out of the drawing room and Betty scurried in from the kitchen.

"Why, George, what a surprise and a pleasure! Come in, come in. Compliments of the season to you. Oh, this is Jack Dance, who's staying with us over the holiday. Jack, this is Mr. Thompson, one of the best lawyers in town. Thanks, Betty…Jack beat you to it again!"

Mr. Thompson smiled at the lad.

"New doorman, eh?" he said, shaking hands. They chuckled as Joe led the way into the drawing room.

"Come and say hello to Susan Ann. She'll be delighted you're here. Can I get you something to keep out the chill?"

"As a matter of fact, I've come to see you on business, Joe. I know it's an odd time for that, but this is a serious matter – I have something for you. Perhaps we could…" he motioned towards Joe's study.

"Of course," Joe broke in. "Come along. Jack, bring some cider and a couple of glasses will you? Betty doesn't seem to be about."

The two men disappeared into the study, leaving the door ajar. A couple of minutes later Jack entered with his tray and put it down on a table. Joe was standing in front of the crackling fireplace, reading from some paper that Mr. Thompson had obviously just handed to him. His eyes were fixed on the page and there was a smile of amazement on his face.

"Read this, Jack – what do you think?"

Jack was almost out of the room when he heard his name. He ran back in again and took the paper Joe was holding out to him. Mr. Thompson looked on in surprise.

"Hey Joe, I said it's for your eyes alone. I don't think—"

"Don't worry, George. This is my special assistant. And besides, it won't be long before everyone in Nova Scotia will be reading it."

"You mean you'll publish it?" George asked excitedly.

"It'll probably land me in a whole lot of trouble, but I think the time has come. Take this, Jack: what do you think?"

While Joe poured out some Christmas cheer for his friend, Jack took the paper and began to read.

CHAPTER FIVE

THE SMUGGLERS' CELLAR

Mr. Howe: Sir,
Living as I do in a free and intelligent country, and under a consti-
tution which makes our rulers responsible in all matters of govern-
ment, is it not surprising that the people of Halifax should have so
long submitted to the shameful and barefaced taxes which have been
imposed on them year after year?

Jack looked up at Joe, his eyes shining, and then glanced down at the end of the letter. It was signed "The People." He looked over at Mr. Thompson, who placed a finger to his lips. So it was *his* letter! He read on, almost in disbelief. Everything that *The Novascotian* had been hinting at this last year was mentioned here: the unfair taxes, the bribes taken by some of the magistrates, the state of the poor people of the town, the corruption of the police. But these were no hints – they were outright accusations. The letter even suggested that huge sums of money had been taken from the people by the magistrates, to line their own pockets.

"Take it to Mrs. Howe, Jack, right away will you?" said Joe, even before Jack had finished reading.

"Yes sir," said Jack, turning to the door and almost bumping into it from trying to read at the same time. He looked back: "It's wonderful, Mr. Thompson!" he cried, his eyes glowing, and disappeared.

"That's a smart boy," laughed the visitor. "Can he be trusted?"

"With your life, George. He's coming into my office next month, and I expect he'll be writing for us within a year or two.

If the young people coming up are anything like him, Nova Scotia's going to be in safe hands." They sipped their cider, and Mr. Thompson eyed his friend closely.

"So tell me, Joe – will you publish my letter?"

"No, you will not, Joseph Howe!" Mrs. Howe burst angrily into the room, followed by Jack. She was holding the letter in her hand. "You know where this will lead you – straight into Bridewell Jail. Ah, so it's you, George – is this your work again?" She knew that George had already sent a long letter to the paper in the fall, which Joe had published at some risk.

"Look, Susan Ann – " began Joe, but there was no stopping her.

" – Joe, we are having a hard enough time as it is, and this will give those wicked magistrates just what they need. They'll silence you for ever! And why haven't you signed it with your own name, George – tell me that. Because they'll come down on top of you, won't they? Are you expecting Joe to take the heat off you?"

"Not at all, Mrs. Howe," said George. "If Joe publishes this new letter, he has every right to tell them who wrote it. I'm prepared for that. I just feel that if someone doesn't take on that bunch of criminals down at the Town Office, we shall never be free of them. And your paper is the place to start."

The argument went on for some minutes. Finally Mrs. Howe calmed down and was persuaded that the letter simply *must* appear, whatever the risk. Jack, who said nothing but had listened intently, was sent for more glasses and cider so they could raise a toast together. "To 1835!" cried Joe, lifting his glass. "Perhaps Halifax is finally going to take charge of its own affairs."

"To 1835!" said the company.

The letter was folded up and Joe gave it to Jack, with instructions to take it to the printshop first thing the morning after Christmas. He ran to his room and put the letter carefully away in a drawer. It was his first real job for Joe Howe, and he was proud of the responsibility – something that Joe saw and took note of.

And then came Christmas. It was everything Jack had hoped it would be. There was a great goose to eat, and nuts and fruit, and sugar candies. There were fires in every room, and candles and beautiful oil lamps lighting up the halls. There was holly over the pictures, and mistletoe to kiss under, and streamers along the tables. There were games and races, and singing and dancing and gifts. Everyone received just one gift, and Jack – oh joy! – found himself the owner of a brand new toboggan, brightly painted in red and green. Mrs. Dance was even able to join the company for a little while, and it did her a world of good. All in all, it was a wonderful time!

After Christmas lunch, when the children – who had been up since before dawn – had been sent off to their rooms for a nap, and even the grown-ups were opening their collars and getting sleepy, Jack put on his cap, long muffler, gloves and boots, picked up his new toboggan, and let himself out into the snowy street. It had suddenly turned very cold: the sidewalks were icy, and the boys of the town had already brought out their butchers' trays and boards and started racing crazily down the steep streets leading to the harbour. Jack watched them enviously, but he treasured his new gift too much to chance it on those terrifying slopes. So he turned and tramped up to Citadel Hill, where the soldiers of the barracks had set up a slide for the children of the garrison and their friends.

He was just climbing back up for his third slide when he looked up and saw a big toboggan with three boys on board hurtling towards him. He jumped out of the way, and as they passed by there was a nasty shout. "Watch it Jackyboy! You'll get it one of these days!" It was Harry Hemple. The boys laughed and sniggered as they whizzed away down to the bottom, where they fell off in a heap and started ragging each other. Jack continued up the hill. Were they going to wait for him when he came down again? But when he turned round at the top he saw them being called into the street below, where a sleigh had stopped to pick them up.

After a couple more runs, Jack hoisted his toboggan on to his shoulder and set off back to the house. But on a sudden whim he

"WATCH IT JACKYBOY!"

decided to head down towards the harbour. He realized that it was many weeks since he had gone to look out to sea for his father's ship: Christmas Day was a good time to remember his dear dad, he thought.

He soon found himself walking down the very same street where Joe Howe had rescued him. It had been only six weeks ago, but it seemed as though a whole year had gone by, so much had happened to him since then.

As he drew near to the spot he suddenly caught sight of Ezra, the big burly man who had nearly knocked him over. Jack retreated quickly into a dark doorway to watch. Ezra was at the gate of the yard where he had been delivering that day. He was with another man Jack hadn't seen before, who seemed to be putting some money into Ezra's hand, looking around to be sure he wasn't watched. He was dressed all in black and carried a thick cane: there were wisps of grey hair showing under his hat. Ezra counted out the coins suspiciously and then disappeared inside, returning a minute later with a wicker basket holding six tall bottles, which he handed over.

"And wish yer maister a Merry Christmas from me, will yer, Cliff? He should be merry enough with these insoide 'im!" And they both laughed. Cliff took a dark cloth from his pocket, placed it over the bottles, nodded to Ezra and took off down to Water Street, where he turned south. He walked with a pronounced limp, looking like a scrawny black insect against the snow.

As soon as Ezra had gone back inside, Jack darted out from the doorway and followed "Cliff," as Ezra had called him. He kept well behind, and when Cliff paused to get his breath Jack paused too, looking into a store window, hiding behind a cart, or pretending to tie his bootlace. Cliff made his way past Keith's Brewery, then up the hill again. But all of a sudden he disappeared. Jack ran to where he had been one minute earlier. No sign of him among the Christmas strollers, or in the doorways. Then Jack noticed a small grey door in the grey wall of the big merchants' warehouse that lined the street on that side. He looked round to make sure no one was watching him, then went up to the door and gently pushed it. It gave to his touch, and he stepped cautiously inside.

At first it was so dark he could see nothing. But he heard shouts and laughter coming from somewhere, and as his eyes grew accustomed to the light he could make out a twisted staircase going down towards some kind of cellar. He started down the stairs, but all of a sudden the door at the bottom opened and a shaft of light hit the steps. He jumped back into a corner as a couple of men emerged from the cellar and came rapidly up the stairs.

"I reckon we're on the tide here, Pat," said one to the other as they climbed. "Once we get the jail contract we can sit back and just watch the money rolling in."

"And nobody the wiser," said the other. "Not even Joe Howe!" They chuckled. Jack held his breath and shrank into the wall as best he could. The men were so close he could smell drink on their breath. He tried to make out their faces but could see nothing until they opened the little door to the outside. Jack caught just a glimpse of a bright red kerchief round the neck of one man. The other seemed to be dressed like a gentleman, and carried a cane. The door closed and it was dark again. He was safe.

Jack waited a little then tiptoed towards the door. But he had a second thought. What was going on down there in the cellar? There was still laughter and even some singing coming from below. He took a deep breath and began creeping down the stone steps. At the bottom was a makeshift door covered in sacking. He pushed it open just a crack and looked through.

What a sight met his eyes! The cellar was huge, with a high, vaulted ceiling and stone walls stretching back into the distance. Along the walls were shelves and on them – he could hardly believe it – was every kind of object he could imagine: boxes of all shapes and sizes, huge Chinese pots, cages with parrots and monkeys chattering in them, bolts of silk every colour of the rainbow, wooden sculptures, chinaware, wheels, sacks…and in the middle of the room a huge table of rough pine sitting on trestles: it was twenty times bigger that any table he had ever seen in his

life. Around the table sat a crowd of people: soldiers in bright red uniforms, their collars open; women with garishly painted faces; sailors, carters, lascars from the ships in the port. They were drinking and singing and laughing, and the noise was deafening. In the middle of the table, at the far end, sat a big, fat man in a cutaway coat and a blue stock around his neck. He was red-faced and toothless and was smoking a long pipe, which he took out of his mouth every once in a while to take a great swill of ale from a glass mug beside him.

Jack took in everything he could see, and tried specially to fix in his memory the faces of that swaying, baying crowd of people. Suddenly he saw a big, blowsy woman with a tall, empty pitcher in her hand coming right up to the door where he was hiding. He took a leap back, turned, and raced up the stairs, his toboggan still on his shoulder and crashing into the wall as he ran.

"Come back, you!" he heard her shouting. "What are you doin' here, yer varmint! Come down 'ere!" But Jack was gone like lightning, through the little grey door and up the street, as fast as he could go. As he turned the corner he glanced back. The woman who had spotted him was pointing in his direction, and a couple of men were shaking their fists and started after him, shouting. He sped out of sight. But he was not too scared. No one knew the back alleys and little lanes of Halifax like Jack. He realized his toboggan would give him away, so he dropped it into some bushes behind a wall. He would pick it up later. He could run that much faster without it, and soon he was safe from being pursued, his tracks swallowed up in the ice of the sidewalks.

After waiting for a few minutes under a group of trees heavy with snow, he strolled back to Joe Howe's house, and was there in time for a cup of tea and a large slice of pound cake. He was happy to be back in the warm, happy world of the Howe family.

"Where have you been?" said Mrs. Howe. "We were looking for you to play blindman's buff."

"Oh, I went for a slide on the hill," replied Jack, innocently enough. He was longing to tell Joe what had happened, but first he had to think about it. What actually *had* happened, and what did it mean? After supper he said goodnight to his mother, who had gone to bed early, and climbed the stairs to his attic room. He lay back on his cot and thought.

That man Cliff with the limp must have been buying rum from Ezra, and taking it in those bottles to that strange cellar. Was he selling it there? Or perhaps he was just dropping in for a drink himself before taking the rum somewhere else? And who was that big red-faced man in the cutaway coat? He looked like a nasty piece of work, no mistake. And the cellar with all those goods stored along the walls: surely they were brought by ship from foreign places, and had been smuggled in, avoiding customs duties and taxes. Someone was obviously making a lot of money, and illegally.

There was a loud knock at his door, and Edward and Ellen burst in, crying, "Come on Jack, we're waiting for you. We're playing charades and you're on our team!" Edward took Jack's hand and dragged him off the bed and down the stairs, and soon Jack was swept up once again in the fun and laughs of the happiest Christmas he ever remembered.

CHAPTER SIX

TOBOGGAN TROUBLE

J ack woke before seven the next morning, splashed some cold water from the wash-stand basin on to his face and hands, and was soon dressed and ready. He went to his drawer, took out Mr. Thompson's letter and read it again. He especially liked the part that read: "Is it not known that at least 1000 pounds is drawn annually from the pockets of the poor and distressed, and pocketed by men whose services the country might well spare?"

Jack thought of poor Miss Hogg and the money she was still owed. And he thought too of Mr. Hemple and of yesterday's adventure. He hadn't had time to tell Joe Howe about it yet, but perhaps there would be a moment today.

He folded the letter again, and put it carefully in the inside pocket of his jacket. Then he skipped downstairs two at a time to the main landing, and more slowly down the curving staircase to reach the hall. Betty was clearing up the plates and glasses and wrappings from the day before, and in the dining-room Susan Ann was already sitting, eating some toast and drinking tea. She had balanced a ledger on her knee and was checking some figures when he came in.

"Ah, hello Jack," she said with a smile. "You're up early!"

"Yes, I have a job to do right away," replied Jack, walking through to the kitchen to get his coat and cap.

"You must eat some breakfast first, dear," she said firmly. "Here, come and sit."

Jack was eager to be off, but he headed back to the table and sat beside Susan Ann, who helped him to a bowl of porridge.

"So what happened yesterday afternoon?" she asked, as she passed him the milk pitcher and the jar of sticky molasses.

"What do you mean, Mrs. Howe?" he stammered, and felt himself blushing a little.

"I saw a look in your eye when you came back," she said. "You were excited in a sort of secret way. You may have gone sliding, but something else happened too. And where was your toboggan when you came back?" Her eyes were twinkling, and it was clear she was not scolding him in any way. But she was showing she had noticed, and was encouraging him to tell her his secret – if he wanted to. Did he want to? He wasn't sure. He loved this kind, strong woman who had welcomed him into her house like one of her own children, and he certainly didn't want to tell her lies.

"Well," he said slowly. "I – I saw the man Mr. Howe rescued me from the day we met, and, well, he seemed to be doing something suspicious. But then someone saw me watching that man, and he started towards me. I ran, and he chased after me. I had to throw my toboggan over a hedge 'cos it was slowing me down. I got away, and I'm going back to get my toboggan today."

"Look, just you be careful, my dear," she said, after listening to his account. "There are some shady folks around this town, and we can't have you getting caught up in their goings-on. Your mother will never forgive us if we don't look after you."

"Yes, Mrs. Howe," he answered meekly. Of course he would take care of himself, but he had no intention of putting a stop to his adventures. Joe Howe had particularly asked him to keep his eyes and ears open, and that was what he was doing.

He washed down his porridge with a glass of apple juice.

"May I leave the table, now?" he asked politely.

"Of course – away you go. Mr. Howe's already at the office, I think. Tell him what you told me, won't you?"

"Yes, ma'am, I will."

Jack found his coat, cap and muffler in the hall among the jumble of family hats, scarves and overcoats. He let himself out through the kitchen, giving a quick kiss to Hannah as he went, and pulling the heavy door closed behind him.

"That's one special lad ain't he, Betty," said Hannah with a smile.

"I reckon," said Betty shortly.

It was a bright sunny day at last, after days of heavy snow-clouds sweeping in from the ocean, and Jack couldn't help pausing for a minute to enjoy the sight of the sunshine lighting up the white of the snow, and the sweet blue sky above Citadel Hill. Then he turned into the offices of *The Novascotian*, which were alongside the Howes' home.

"We've been waiting twenty minutes, young man: where have you been?" asked Joe Howe, already in his shirtsleeves and writing at his desk.

"I'm sorry, sir," said Jack meekly, handing over the precious letter. He didn't like to say that he had been delayed by Mrs. Howe.

"Rob Woollings!" cried Joe, still writing. In a few seconds Rob came in, wearing his printer's apron and rubbing his ink-stained hands on a cloth.

"Take this to Mr. McNab. Tell him I want it set up just as soon as he can. Strike it off for me the moment it's ready — I want to have a look at it in print. Hurry along!" Rob snatched up the letter and disappeared at the double, back into the print shop.

"So you'll be joining us here in a few more days, Jack," said Joe, turning to the boy. "What are you going to do with your time until then?"

"Do you remember, sir, when you told me I should keep an ear to the ground?" Joe nodded. "Well, I've been doing that. And I've seen a few things…" Jack proceeded to tell him all about his adventure on Christmas Day: about Ezra, and Cliff the insect man, and the cellar with all its treasures and dubious characters. Joe listened intently to the end.

"Would they recognize you if they saw you again?" he asked.

"I don't think so. I was far away when they looked up the street. I think there's something bad going on, don't you?"

"Sounds like it. Now listen, Jack. What you have told me is very interesting indeed. It could be important. But I beg you to be careful."

"But didn't you tell me the other day that sometimes we have to take risks, sir, if we want to do anything worth doing?"

Joe looked down at the boy, his eyes fearless and a little smile playing on his lips.

"You be careful is all I'm saying, Jack," he said, smiling back. "Your mother would never forgive me if you got hurt." Hadn't Mrs. Howe said exactly those same words? "Besides, you'll be taking her back to your home in a day or two, and you're all she has, you know."

"I'll take care of myself, sir – and of her too," said Jack.

"All right. Off with you then, I have an editorial to finish. Make the most of your holiday, because you'll be working hard the moment the new year comes. And spend a bit of time with the children whenever you can. It means a lot to them."

"I will, sir. Just one thing, sir: why did you give me Mr. Thompson's letter to bring to the office? You could have done it yourself."

"I wanted to see if you would remember, that's all. I want to be able to trust you with serious things when you work here. Understand?"

"Yes, sir."

"Now away you go."

Jack put his cap and gloves back on and stepped out into the street.

"I'll fetch my toboggan for a start," he thought. He began whistling as he ambled along, delighted by his chat with Joe. He could hardly wait until New Year's Day, when he'd be walking in to take his new job. Before then, of course, he'd have to move his mother back home. She was almost back to her old form, and Jack was so happy to see her up and about, taking an interest in everything around her. He was even looking forward to the move, and to settling back into his tiny room in William Alley.

Jack reached the stone wall at the corner of Salter Street, where he had thrown his toboggan. He looked round. Rich folks bundled up in furs were driving past in sleighs drawn by sleek horses. Others were strolling around enjoying the sun. Several merchants were hurrying towards the wharves to meet a newly arrived vessel from Britain. An officer was walking stiffly downhill in the same direction, perhaps to pick up a new detachment of soldiers. No one was taking any notice of a boy idling on the street corner.

In one lithe movement Jack vaulted lightly over the wall behind him, landing in the snow the other side. But where was his toboggan? Not where he had thrown it the day before. He searched around in the undergrowth. No sign of it. He pushed his way through the snow-laden bushes and found himself at the end of a big backyard, with steps up to a terrace and a tall stone house facing him. Better not be seen here, he thought. But suddenly something caught his eye. At the corner of the garden, in a patch of ground bare of snow, he saw the cold ashes of a bonfire – and, on top of it, the remains of his beloved toboggan. Its red-painted front was blistered and charred. The rest was gone – just a heap of dead embers.

Jack let out a cry of anger, and ran to get a better look.

He wasn't sure what happened next: suddenly, for no reason, he tripped and fell. Then he felt a sharp blow on his head. He remembered no more.

CHAPTER SEVEN

JACK FINDS OUT A THING OR TWO

W hen Jack came to, still lying on the snow where he had
fallen, he put his hand to his aching head. Then he
opened his eyes, and saw, standing above him in a circle, three
boys and a girl. They had sticks in their hands. One of the boys
was Harry Hemple. They were all laughing, but they looked
threatening enough, and Jack was scared. The important thing,
Jack knew, was not to show it.

"Hello, you folks," he said lightly, and started to get up.

"Hold on, you little worm – not so fast," said Harry, knocking
him down again with his knee.

Jack looked round at the other boys and at the girl, who looked
just as menacing as the others.

"So, did you burn up my toboggan? What a brave thing to do,
that was," said Jack. "What's your next dirty trick? Set fire to me
too?"

"Maybe," said the girl, with a sneer. Jack stared piercingly at her,
and her eyes dropped to the ground. She was younger than Harry,
but looked enough like the bully to be his sister, perhaps.

"You're a little sneak, Dance," said Harry. "You may think you've
landed on your feet getting a job with that busybody Joe Howe,
but just you wait: if you get caught up in his affairs, your life won't
be worth living. Get that, Jackyboy?" And he tapped the end of his
stick on Jack's head. Jack lost his calm and grabbed hold of the stick,
pulling sharply so that Harry lost his balance. Jack bounced to his
feet and started to take off towards the wall. But the other two boys
barred his way, and one punched him on the shoulder. Angered by

the blow he swung round and gave his assailant a good knock on the nose. The boy cried out and put his hand to his face, while the other raised his stick to bring it down on Jack's head. But just at that moment there was a shout from the terrace.

"Harry! Boys! What's going on there?"

"We've got the intruder, father! It's Mr Howe's little spy again. Hit him, Peter, go on!"

"That's enough of that. You come back to the house at once – all of you. And bring the lad with you. Gently now."

Jack looked up towards the terrace to see who owned that big, booming voice. But the little gang surrounded him and pushed him forward over the snow. Jack's heart sank, and he started thinking: Ever since I first met Joe Howe I seem to have had one scary moment after another. And now this. Perhaps Miss Pringle and Hemple were right. Perhaps Joe Howe is just a trouble-maker, and I should look for work somewhere else. Perhaps.

They climbed the steps to the terrace and came to a French door, which stood open to receive them. Harry pushed Jack ahead of him through the door.

They were in a large, high hallway, and there in the middle stood the owner of the booming voice. A huge man, with greying hair, a big red nose, piercing eyes, and hands like frying pans they were so wide and strong.

"You boys leave us – this moment, Harry. And you too, Lucy – what'yer doing anyway, playing around with sticks? Go and change and practise y'r piano – or I'll be after yer."

Lucy threw her stick angrily on the floor and flounced upstairs. She paused to look down at Jack. Jack looked back at her, and thought – for a moment – that he saw someone quite different from the mean little girl he had met in the backyard. She seemed frightened, and small. She opened her mouth to speak, but thought better of it and ran up the stairs and out of sight. Harry picked up her stick and said: "Come on, gang. We've done our job. Let's go." They trooped out, looking back smugly at Jack as they went.

"Come with me, boy," said Mr. Hemple, as he led the way into his den. Jack gazed about him as they went. It was a luxurious house, with fine English furniture and carpets, and a grandfather clock ticking contentedly in the hall. In Mr. Hemple's study there was a big cherrywood desk littered with papers. "Don't worry about y'r boots. We have people to clean up. Sit there." He pointed to a chair by the window.

"I'll stand, sir, if you don't mind."

"Please y'rself. Now what's y'r name?"

"Jack, sir."

"And what would you be doin' in me backyard, Jack? Speak up."

"I wanted to get my toboggan back, sir."

"And why would y'r toboggan be sittin' in me backyard, Jack?"

"I threw it there, on Christmas Day."

"You threw it there did you? And why would you do that, Jack?"

"I was in a hurry, sir. It was slowing me down."

Jack saw the way Mr. Hemple's questions were heading. It wouldn't be long before he would be asked what he was running away from. So he went on the attack:

"Why was it burnt, sir? They had no right to do that."

"They didn't do it," said Mr. Hemple grimly. "Did it meself. Cup o' lamp oil and it went up like a firework." He turned suddenly on Jack and glared down at him, shouting: "I won't have people comin' on to me property! I won't have them snoopin' around like damn insecks. I won't have it, see?"

"I was just coming to collect my toboggan. I wasn't doing anything wrong. And you burnt it up — you just burnt it up!" Jack looked angrily back up at him, which made him more furious still.

"Don't you dare shout at me, you little varmint! Another word out of you and — "

At that moment there was a knock at the door.

"Come on in then!" barked Mr. Hemple.

The door opened, and in came a grey-haired man dressed all in black. He walked with a limp, and it didn't take Jack long to recognize the man who had picked up bottles of liquor from Ezra, then disappeared into that amazing cellar on Salter Street. What was his name? Ah yes – Cliff.

"Excuse me, Mr. Hemple, sir," said Cliff, "there's a couple of sailors at the back door be wanting payment for something or other. They said you would be expecting them. I told them – "

"Never mind what you told them," snarled Mr. Hemple, angry at being interrupted, but flustered too at the news. "Wait here, boy – and don't you stir, mind me?"

Jack nodded, and Mr. Hemple hurried out followed by Cliff, who turned to give the boy a nasty look as he went out.

Jack heard the two men walk through to the back of the house. A door closed, and everything fell silent but for the ticking of the clock in the hall.

For a few seconds Jack stood there, trying to decide whether to make a run for it. But then he had a better idea. He stole cautiously over to the big desk where Mr. Hemple's papers lay scattered. There were letters and receipts and bills in untidy piles. He picked up one invoice, then another. They were bills for food and liquor, one for repair of a sled, another for carpet-boots. Jack didn't know much about business affairs, but he used to help his mother with her bills, so he was able to understand what he was reading: "To His Worship the Hon. W. Hemple, Esq., Magistrate. Item: 2 turkeys, plucked and trussed: 2 shillings" – and so on. Nothing much of interest here. His eye wandered to a set of papers under a half-empty wineglass. After making sure the coast was still clear he moved the glass aside and picked up the papers. On top was a letter addressed to Mr. Hemple. He scanned it, but then went back to the top and read it thoroughly, every word.

Your Worship

It has now been three months and two days since we made our agreement regarding the rum and brandy shipments. I have carried out my side of the bargain, and have made sure that my vessels brought in their cargo safe from Boston, and up the Bay of Fundy to Windsor. I then arranged for the casks to be transported by horse and sleigh to Halifax on the postroad. This was a dangerous game I can tell you, and had to be undertaken at night, hiding in the forest by day. My men succeeded however, and on October 12th brought the goods to George Street where your storeman Ezra took delivery.

Mr. Hemple, sir, since that time I have received not one shilling for the shipment, nor do I have any guarantee that your promise of paying off the customs and excise officers is being kept: they are keeping a close watch on my ship wherever I sail. I also have evidence that you have been disposing of the liquor to your friends for a good price. If you do not furnish the money owing to me by Christmas Eve, I shall send men to your door to obtain it – something I am sure you do not wish for.
Your obedient servant,
Hosea Watts, Capt.
On board Saucy Jane, lying off Annapolis Royal

Now, Jack did not know very much about imports and exports, but it didn't take much guesswork to realize what the letter was all about. Mr. Hemple, one of the city magistrates, was directly involved in smuggling! Jack started breathing fast from sheer excitement. He shuffled quickly through the other papers in the same pile and they were all invoices and receipts – except that the items received and billed for were all marked as "pitch" or "molasses." He was just picking up another bill at the bottom of the pile when he heard the door opening out in the hall. Like lightning he stuffed the bills back together, and then the letter he had read. Steps were crossing the hall as he moved the wineglass back onto the pile. At the very last instant he decided to pull the letter out again, nearly turning the glass over and spilling some drops of wine on the desk. As he ran back to where he had been standing he jammed the letter into his pocket.

Mr. Hemple appeared a second later. He looked very angry, and seemed almost to have forgotten that Jack was waiting for him.

"Oh yes – you. Now listen here. Harry tells me that you work for Joe Howe. Is this true?"

"No, not yet. I start on New Year's Day."

"Well, I'll tell you one thing here and now: if ever that meddling Howe prints anything that he gets from your pryin' and snoopin', I tell you now, you'll be roast pork quick as a shot – is that clear?"

"I hear what you're saying, sir."

"Don't give me that lah-di-dah stuff! Your life's goin' to be on the line from here on in. D'you understand? We know where you are, where you live, the streets where you walk, everythin' about you. So you'd best watch it, see?"

"If you're threatening me sir, yes, I understand. But if I'm working for Mr Howe you can't expect me not to help him when he's trying to clean up this town. That'll be my job. I have to do my job."

Mr. Hemple grabbed Jack by the collar and pulled him up almost off his feet. "D'you understand, yer rogue?" he hissed. "You'll be roast pork."

Jack struggled to get free but the man was big and powerful. He made to strike the boy, then thought better of it.

"Get out of here. Go on – get out," said Mr. Hemple, and still holding Jack's collar dragged him back into the hallway and towards the front door of the house. He opened the door and threw Jack out on to the snow-covered steps. "You watch it, lad!" he said, and banged the door shut.

Jack picked himself up and looked back fiercely at the tall stone house towering over him. There was a number on the door in brass: 17. He took note of it and turned away. He was feeling thoroughly miserable. He had a sore head. He had been bullied by Harry and his gang. He had been shouted at by that horrible man Mr. Hemple. And worst of all, he had lost his beautiful new toboggan. What bad luck to have hidden it right in Mr. Hemple's back yard! He was going to have to explain all that to Mr. and Mrs. Howe. They would be certain to want to know everything, and he had no idea how Mr. Howe would take it. But then there was Mr. Hemple's letter he had in his pocket. Surely Mr. Howe would like to see that? But maybe not. It was difficult to know.

Back at the house, he waited until after the midday meal, and was able to get Mr. and Mrs. Howe together and alone as they sipped their tea. He told them everything that had happened that morning. They listened with more and more alarm. When he told them how he was left alone and had read Mr. Hemple's mail, he fished the stolen letter out of his pocket and handed it to them. They read it in silence, and then looked at one another without a word. Joe folded the letter, stood up and put it on the mantel shelf. For a few seconds there was silence, with Jack looking uneasily from one to the other.

"Susan Ann," said Joe at length, "I am taking off from the office this afternoon. Jack and I are going skating. You have skates, Jack?"

"They're at home, sir."

"I expect I'll be able to find another pair in the closet. Come on, finish your tea and get your boots on. Susan Ann, send Betty over to the office and tell them I won't be back in until this evening."

"I'll drop by myself, Joe," she replied. "I need to go over some proofs with Angus McNab anyway."

Half an hour later Joe Howe was striding up Sackville Street with Jack Dance beside him, confused to be taking off so suddenly, and not sure why. Neither Joe nor his wife had yet said a word to him after hearing about this latest adventure, and he was still not certain whether he had displeased them or not. Time would tell — maybe.

CHAPTER EIGHT

SKATES AND WARNINGS

"This is my home turf," said Joe Howe suddenly, after they had been hiking for twenty minutes down the snowy country lane leading to the North-West Arm. "I was born on the shore right over there – you see the little house by the cove? That was ours." Jack looked over to his left and saw a tiny cottage with a shingle roof, and smoke trailing from the chimney. "When I was your age," Joe went on, "we would fish and swim and row here every summer day. And in the winter we'd never be off the ice."

"The Arm," as they called it, was a long, narrow inlet of the ocean, which thrust in behind the spit of land on which Halifax stood. Some winters it never froze over, but this year, with frosty nights since early November, people were already sliding and skating, and as Joe and Jack approached the edge they could hear shouts and laughing. A little way along, a group of boys were playing hurley, sending a small, flat disc scudding over the ice. Jack had never seen anyone move so fast as these players, weaving and turning after the disc, and racing with it to the goal.

"Come on, Jack, let's get our skates on and have a fling. It's been a year or two since I've done this, and you may have to pick me up a few times."

They sat down on a bench, strapped on their skates, and took off over the bay. A breeze had picked up from the ocean, and dark grey clouds had moved in and were racing along the sky. The air was cold and bracing, but with their vigorous exercise it didn't take long to warm up. There were couples of all ages skating arm in arm, children being coaxed along the ice by their parents, and a few

speeding, solitary skaters who looked as though they were practising for a race to the death. All at once Jack spotted his old schoolfriends Sam and Dick, and skated over to them to exchange news and Christmas greetings. He was dying to tell them of all his adventures, but was wise enough to keep them to himself. Every so often he looked round for Joe Howe, who was greeting acquaintances at every turn but seemed always to be looking over in Jack's direction.

After an hour or so, as the already dull winter light began to fail, Joe called over to Jack and signalled to the little shanty set up on the edge of the bay, where skaters could buy tea or lemon drinks and watch the lively scene. He bought Jack and himself a bun and a hot lemonade, and they sat by the tiny, steamy window.

"You're good on the ice, Jack. Have you been skating long?"

"My dad taught me when I was five. I've been doing it ever since. You're good too, sir!" he added admiringly.

Joe smiled. "Have you played hurley?"

"No, but I'd like to try."

"My apprentices go and play on the weekends. Maybe you'll be able to join them when you start work with me."

"I'd like that very much."

They were chatting easily about ordinary things, but Jack got the feeling that the talk was going to change any minute to something more serious. He wasn't wrong.

"Now look, Jack," said Joe, leaning back in his chair and eyeing the boy closely, "Mrs. Howe and I like you a lot. You may have been wondering why I have taken you under my wing, and I'm going to tell you. You're bright and quick-witted, you're interested in how our little world in Halifax works, and you have a strong sense of right and wrong, which I admire very much. You're brave and resourceful. You're also a loyal person, I believe – loyal to your parents but also to your friends. I like that too."

Jack glowed with pride. To get such high praise from Mr. Howe was a special thing. He kept his eye on his mentor, blushing slightly and taking another bite of his sugar bun. He didn't reply, because he guessed that something else might be coming that wouldn't be so complimentary.

"As I told you, I was raised right here on the Arm. We had very little money, because my father lost everything when he left America and came here after the revolution. All he had was a printing press — it used to belong to Benjamin Franklin, he's told me. So he set up a printing shop in Halifax, and eventually became the King's Printer."

Joe went on to tell Jack how he went to school only in the summer, because of the distance from town; how his father tutored him during the winter, and how they would read Shakespeare and the Bible together; how he started writing poetry as a boy, got a poem printed in the *Gazette* newspaper when he was seventeen, and at one time thought he might want to be a professional poet; how he went to work at Jack's age as a printer's boy at his step-brother's printshop, and then became an apprentice and fell in love with language and the power of the press.

"When I met you, Jack," he went on, "I suppose I saw in you what I was like myself at your age, and decided to see if I could help you. My apprentices are mostly orphans, and I have taken them under my wing for the same reason. And I was right about you! You seem to have the same spirit of adventure that I've always had. Perhaps it came from your seagoing father — what do you think?"

"I don't know, sir: we've never seen very much of him at home."

"Ah, but maybe it's in the blood. Anyway, it's there, and we've been seeing a lot of it these last few days, haven't we. In fact, too much, Jack — too much."

"Yes, sir," Jack responded lamely, not knowing what else to say. Here it comes.

"Now you're starting work at the newspaper next Thursday. On that very day Mr. Thompson's letter is to be printed in the paper, and I have a feeling that things are going to start getting pretty hot for me and for our office. I may be in serious trouble with the rich and powerful who run this country, including the governor himself. And the last thing I need is to have to worry about my printer's devil getting into scrapes on my behalf. Now is that clear, Jack my boy?"

"Yes, it is, sir. But what about Mr. Hemple's smuggling, and all those terrible things going on down on Water Street? Surely that letter was all the evidence you need. Shouldn't he and his friends all be arrested? I don't think – "

"Jack, Jack," interrupted Joe, with a smile at the boy's indignation, "You have to be patient. And you have to know that there is a right time and a wrong time for everything in this world. We are soon going to have a much bigger fight on our hands. Not only Mr. Hemple, but all the other magistrates who run this town of ours may be after my skin by this time next week. If we know they are doing evil things, we need to spring it on them when the moment is ripe, and not a second before. Understand?"

"Yes, sir, I do."

"And by the way – that letter you took…"

"Yes, sir?"

"I've burnt it."

"Oh no! But surely –?"

"You stole it, Jack. You were very resourceful and courageous, but the fact is that it was stolen. I could never produce it in court or anywhere else. And above all it should not be traced back to you. Your life could be in danger."

"Do you think so?" asked Jack, wide-eyed.

"I know it. These people are unscrupulous. They are running a dirty business, and if they get caught they could lose everything. They'll think nothing of cutting your throat in a back-alley. You've already got them angry and suspicious."

Jack was silent. He wasn't exactly afraid, because he always thought he could outwit and outrun just about anyone. But he did realize that he had been putting Joe Howe in a difficult position, and this was something that really bothered him. He frowned and looked down at the table.

"So what should I do?"

"First, I want you to promise me not to go into the streets of the town alone for the next few days, until I feel that the situation has cooled off. Is that clear?"

"Not even for – "

"Not for any reason whatsoever, Jack. Do you promise?"

Jack looked up at the face of his protector. Joe's eyes looked straight back at him, kindly but deadly serious. The boy sighed.

"Yes, sir."

"Good, Jack. I will have Rob Woollings accompany you whenever you need to leave the house. Secondly, after lunch I asked your mother to delay her return home with you until the new year. She's agreed. Third, I want you to forget all about the smuggling ring we have nosed out, and help me deal with some of the bigger problems that may arise once our famous letter is printed. Is that clear?"

"Yes, sir."

" – And by the way, you are one of only three people who know who wrote that letter, and you must never on any account reveal its author. Do you understand?"

"Of course, sir. Anyway, it was written by 'The People,' right?"

"That's right, Jack," said Joe with a smile. "Now, let's pick up our things and go off home. It's almost dark, and I didn't bring a lantern with me."

The two set off back to town. It was by now a very dark night indeed, but Joe had walked and run and snowshoed along that lane so many hundreds of times since boyhood that he could have found his way blindfolded. Besides, there were many other groups making their way home too, singing songs and laughing and playing as they went. Some of them had lanterns to light the path, and occasionally a horse and sleigh glided past with ringing bells, its lamps sending their soft, weaving light over the snow. Joe and Jack were home in plenty of time for dinner.

CHAPTER NINE

THE PRINTER'S DEVIL

J ack had given his word, and during those long days before the new year came he was true to it, although it was almost more than he could bear to look outside day after day and see all the excitement of the street: the sleighs of the rich young people going by with long red ribbons flying behind them in the wind, and boys and girls running and laughing and throwing snowballs, and soldiers marching, and peddlers trudging by with heavy packs of goods on their backs. It was like watching a play, he thought – although he had never been inside a real theatre. He sat with his nose up to the glass in the dining-room for hours at a time, until Edward pulled him away to play hide and seek, or to taste a pie that had just come out of Hannah's oven. Often he would sit with his mother in the parlour and fetch her a cup of tea, then read to her from one of the hundreds of books in Joe Howe's library – especially poetry, which they both loved.

Mrs. Dance was knitting again – a real sign that she was back to her old self! – and while her wooden needles clicked and clacked she listened and watched. Her little boy was growing up. He looked so fine sitting up in the big red chair by the fire, his fiercely grey eyes darting across the page, a slight frown on his face as he concentrated on the words in front of them, and what they meant. She was going to see a lot less of him once he started work, she thought. But she too had come to admire Mr. Howe above anyone in the world, and she reckoned she couldn't be putting Jack into safer hands.

The Howes' big, rambling home was a beautiful place, filled

with people that Jack had come to love almost like his own family. But it was still a sort of prison, and Jack became more and more restless as the days passed, longing for the open air, and even keen to get back home and start his new life at the office. The high point of every day was when the big front door opened and Joe Howe marched in with a cheerful shout: "Hello everyone! Edward, where are you? Ellen my girl! Come give your daddy a kiss! Jack, you rascal, come and take my coat!" And he would stride into the parlour with Edward hanging on to him and little Ellen in his arms. "There you are, Mrs. Dance – how are you feeling? Better? I'm so glad." He turned and called out of the door: "Betty! Is dinner ready? I have to be away again in a jiffy. Susan Ann, where are you, my love?"

Soon they would all be crowded round the dining-room table, with Betty scurrying round serving the food, and Joe talking of the day's events. But these were busy days at the office, and before long, whatever time of day or night, Joe would stand up, wipe his mouth with a napkin, and say, "Well, children, it's back to work." He would kiss Susan Ann goodbye, and stride off into the hall, back out into the snowy street, then into the office two doors down.

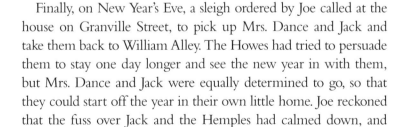

Finally, on New Year's Eve, a sleigh ordered by Joe called at the house on Granville Street, to pick up Mrs. Dance and Jack and take them back to William Alley. The Howes had tried to persuade them to stay one day longer and see the new year in with them, but Mrs. Dance and Jack were equally determined to go, so that they could start off the year in their own little home. Joe reckoned that the fuss over Jack and the Hemples had calmed down, and that he was safe to be out in the streets again. But he begged him to be watchful wherever he went, and Jack promised he would.

Edward and Jack together loaded up the sleigh with Mrs. Dance's sea-chest, and all sorts of gifts that the Howes had showered on them, including pies and stews and custards that

Hannah had made specially the night before. There were tearful goodbyes from the children and Betty and Hannah, a blessing from old Mr. Howe, a hug from Susan Ann, and from Joe a hearty kiss for Mrs. Dance and a vigorous handshake for Jack. "See you tomorrow, Jack!" he said with a smile. And they were off up the street, looking back to see the whole family on the front doorstep waving and blowing kisses.

"I may have been sick to begin with," said Mrs. Dance to Jack as they turned the corner, "but that was the most wonderful time of my life. And it wouldn't have happened without you. Thank you, dear boy!" And she put her arm close around Jack as they glided homewards over the packed snow.

Mrs. Transom had been minding the house while they were away, and they had sent a note that morning asking her to light up the stove, so the kitchen was cosy and warm when they arrived, with floors swept and everything sparkling and clean.

"Remind me to buy Mrs. Transom a gift," said Mrs. Dance. "Such a good friend." But Jack was already upstairs in his room, unpacking his treasures. It was good to be back. Neither of them felt like staying up for the new year – they seemed to have done nothing but celebrate for days! – but as Jack lay in bed he couldn't help imagining the fun back at Granville Street.

꩜

"Six o'clock, Jack!" Mrs. Dance called up the stairs. Jack was up already, and was soon down for a quick wash in the tin basin beside the stove. Then he dressed in his good jacket and breeches, put on his stout boots, ate a few spoonfuls of porridge, threw a scarf around his neck and a cap on his head, gave a hasty kiss to his mother, and was off into the cold and dark of the early morning for the twenty-minute walk to work. In fact, to keep warm he ran most of the way and so arrived early. But the lamps were already burning inside, and as soon as he walked in, there was Joe with Rob Woollings, Mr. McNab and the other apprentices, bundling up the new edition of *The Novascotian* for delivery around the town and all over the countryside.

"Gentlemen," said Joe. "Stop what you're doing for a moment. This is our new printer's devil, Jack Dance. I want you to make him welcome. Jack, you've met Mr. McNab and Rob. These are my apprentices: Peter Black, Jim Reeves and Bill Bates. Boys, look after Jack, will you?" They all shook hands and said they would.

"Jack, your first job will be to deliver the paper. This morning you'll go along with Rob: he will show you the route and all the houses that take our paper. Then in a day or two you'll be doing it on your own. All right?"

"Yes, sir," said Jack, eagerly.

"Now, back to work, all of you!" said Joe, picking up his lists of subscribers.

There were hundreds of papers to deliver, and Rob and Jack, along with the other apprentices, came back several times for new bundles, delivering them to different sections of the town. Mr. McNab gave Rob and Jack two or three more lots, packaged up to take to the market slip, where they would be put on board the *Sir Charles Ogle*, the new steamboat ferry plying to Dartmouth, and on to the packet boats for delivery to all the coastal towns round the shore of Nova Scotia: Sidney, Liverpool, Shelburne, Yarmouth, Annapolis Royal and Digby. The papers for Windsor and Horton were put into mailbags and delivered to the post office, which sent a rider off across the hills to these settlements on the old post road.

"Do all these people read *The Novascotian?*" asked Jack, in won-derment. "They surely do," said Rob. "Mr Howe's been travelling round the country every summer selling subscriptions. He's famous, you know!"

❧

By the time they had delivered the last packages of papers it was late in the morning. As Rob and Jack came away from the pier and started walking through the market, they noticed a group of merchants outside the Exchange Coffee House talking excitedly among themselves. Several of them were holding copies of *The Novascotian* in their hands, and showing them around.

"Do you see that, Rob?" murmured Jack. "They've read the letter."

"Seems like it," said Rob. "Look over there." A store clerk was standing on a fruitbox reading from the paper to a knot of fishermen and dock workers, who were shouting and laughing and applauding at every sentence. As the boys watched, a party of soldiers with rifles at the ready marched through the market-place under the orders of an officer, who was red-faced and flustered, clutching his pistol and looking around as though a revolution was about to begin.

"Let's go back by Government House where the governor lives, and see what's going on there," said Rob, and they turned south on Water Street. As they walked, boys were running in different directions carrying copies of the paper, and folk were clustered at almost every corner, some of them quiet and grim-looking, others breaking out into guffaws and cheers. Hearing the bells of a sleigh behind them, they turned just in time to see its lead horse take the corner on the way up to Province House.

"That's Mr. Hemple," said Jack, who had dodged quickly behind a barrel to avoid being seen.

"How do you know?" asked Rob, gazing after the sleigh as it climbed the hilly street.

"Oh, I met him once," said Jack, "And his son Harry was at school with me."

"Looks like a pretty nasty man," said Rob.

"He is," said Jack shortly.

Around Government House, as Rob had guessed, there was hustle and bustle. A senior officer – he looked like a general – had just arrived to pay a visit to Governor Campbell, with a platoon of soldiers and several cavalrymen accompanying his sleigh. Other men in military uniform were coming and going, some of them running and carrying dispatches in their hands. Three men whose rich clothes suggested they might be members of the King's

Council walked past the boys in a great hurry, talking through clenched teeth, their greatcoats billowing behind them. Two women dressed in rich furs stopped at the door in a tiny but handsome sleigh, and as their driver helped them down Jack could see they were crying. One had the newspaper in her hand, and they clasped on to each other tearfully as they walked up the steps and into the magnificent house.

∽

"We'd better get back," said Jack. Rob nodded, and they trotted back through the streets, noting wherever they went that the whole town was in a blaze of excitement. As they turned the corner into Granville Street, Jack clutched Rob's arm and pointed. A group of men were throwing snowballs at the windows of *The Novascotian* and jeering – one had even thrown a rock, which smashed a window pane. A couple of sailors tried to grab the men, and a crowd was gathering. The boys raced towards the office, and just as they arrived the door opened, and out stepped Joe Howe. A loud cheer went up from the by-standers as he came in view, a tall, burly figure in his shirtsleeves, and with an utterly fearless smile on his face. He strode over to the struggling men in the street.

"Come, friends, let's not fight," he said. "Let them go, boys. These fellows seem to want to tell me something and I'm happy to listen to them. Ezra, do you have something to say to me? What about you, Silver? Look, I don't mind snowballs, but I'd rather you said it with words than with rocks. Come on into the office and let's chat."

But the men were in no mood to chat. They were a rough lot, headed up by the same Ezra and Silver that Jack had run into all those weeks before, and most of them could probably not even read. They had obviously been sent on this mission by their bosses, without even knowing why. They looked sulkily at Joe, then at the jeering crowd. After hesitating a moment, they turned tail and slunk away down the street, muttering among themselves.

"COME, FRIENDS, LET'S NOT FIGHT."

The crowd cheered, and one or two threw snowballs at the backs of the departing rioters, then took turns shaking Joe's hand.

"You've done a great thing for Halifax, Joe," said one. "Watch your back, Joe," warned another. "That's all I'll say."

"It's the happiest day of my life," said a big, crinkly-faced woman with wispy hair and shining eyes, hugging Joe and planting an enthusiastic kiss on his cheek. Joe chuckled good-naturedly, and turned to the crowd.

"Thank you, all of you. We might need your support these next few weeks. And then again, we might not! I've never seen anything stir these magistrates out of their sleep before, and maybe it'll be the same this time. Let's all go home now and look after each other. Happy New Year!"

"Happy New Year, Joe!" shouted the voices from the crowd in return. Slowly, the group dispersed, still talking and laughing.

∾

Jack had watched all this with amazement. He had come to know Joe Howe as a family man and even as a friend, but he had never seen him face a crowd. How could he have dared to go out in front of that mob of roughnecks, and talk to them in such a friendly way that they were disarmed and helpless in his hands? "I must learn to be like that," he thought to himself, as he and Rob walked through the door to report on what they had seen in the town. Joe listened intently to their story.

"Thank'ee boys, thank'ee," he said at last. "It's good to know. We do seem to have made a few of them sit up and think. And now – to work again!"

CHAPTER TEN
—————————

AN UNEXPECTED FRIEND

"To work again!" Jack heard that a lot in the next weeks. Joe was always ready for a laugh and a chat with every one of his staff, and then: "To work again!" he would say, and everyone would bend once more over their type trays and presses. Joe Howe was tireless, and he expected everyone else to be the same. He wrote constantly – nearly all the articles in the paper, as well as the poems and essays, came from his pen. But somehow he found time once a day to gather the apprentices in his office and give them a lesson about one thing or another: how the politics of Nova Scotia worked, or the way the great British Empire was run, or what the job of a newspaper editor should be. "Always ask yourself: 'What is right?'" he would say: "'What is just? And what is for the public good?' That's the only important thing in our profession."

Sometimes they would take a break from politics, and read a scene from Shakespeare together. At the end of each session they would have a discussion, sometimes lame, sometimes lively. Then Joe would look at the clock on the mantel and call out, "All right – that's enough, boys: to work again!"

As mere printer's devil, Jack was left out of these meetings, but he looked so forlorn at missing them that one day Joe told him to get along in with the others and he scampered into the office excitedly. At first he was shy to be there. But Rob and the other boys welcomed him, and it wasn't long before he shone above them all in his knowledge, his sharp wit and his way of putting things. "You should be doing the talks, not Mr. Howe," said Bill

Bates admiringly. Bill was the simplest of them all, and a lot of it went above his head, but he could tell a bright light when he saw it, and young Jack was a bright light.

∽

Some weeks had gone by, and Jack had settled happily into his job. He swept the office every day and the printshop twice a week. He filled the oil lamps and the inkwells, and sharpened pens and dusted off old Will Shakespeare in his corner. He took letters and notes all round town for Joe, collected paper from the stationers, and brought bread and cheese and beer from the tavern for Mr. McNab when he was working late at the presses. And once a week he spent the morning delivering *The Novascotian* – on his own route now, which made him very proud. Joe always gave him a copy to take home to his mother, who no longer had to buy it – just as well, because her employers had refused to have her back after her illness: "We're just worried about our children catching it," said the master's wife spitefully, showing her the door. Luckily, a mysterious package had recently arrived addressed to Mrs. Dance and apparently from overseas. Inside she found ten golden guineas! It was enough to keep the two of them for a whole year, even without Jack's wages, which he faithfully turned over to his mother every Friday.

"Please don't go out to work, Mother," said Jack. "I may be an apprentice soon, and if times get hard I can always live at the shop like Rob and Bill and the others."

"Well, for the moment I'll stay at home," replied Mrs. Dance gratefully. "There's so much to do." Both of them of course secretly wondered whether the gold coins had been sent by Captain Dance, and whether this meant he was still alive. But it was too painful for them to talk about.

∽

After the first flurry of excitement on New Year's Day, the town had calmed down—in fact the whole storm seemed to have blown over, although the rumour was going about that the magistrates had asked the governor to have Joe Howe arrested and tried for sedition and for stirring up the people to rebel against the king and his government. It was now a month since the letter had been published. So far the governor had taken no action.

"Things seem to be quiet," said Mrs. Howe on one of her frequent visits to the office to gather up receipts and invoices for the ledger.

"Ominously quiet," said Joe, looking up from his desk. Jack piped up:

"I've heard the magistrates want to murder you, sir."

"Oh you have, have you?" responded Joe, with a surprised smile on his face. "And where would you have heard that silly story?"

"…In the town, sir. On my rounds."

"Oh Jack," said Mrs. Howe, shaking her head.

"So you're getting back into your old eavesdropping habits, are you, Jack?" said Joe. "Remember what I said: be careful."

"Oh I am, sir," said Jack, excusing himself quickly from the room: "I wouldn't run any risks, sir."

Now perhaps this wasn't strictly true. The day before, when he had been delivering his papers as usual, Jack suddenly had the feeling that he was being followed. He looked round. There was no one in sight. He walked on and turned again. There was a postman at the house close by, delivering letters, and a dog was yapping as it chased a terrified tabby-cat over the snow-banks piled up on the side of the street, but no other sign of life.

Jack was just a little frightened, but excited too, so when he had delivered his last paper on that round, he decided to play a trick on his tracker, and ducked suddenly into a side alley. A baker's van was drawn up beside the walkway, its horse's breath steaming in the cold air. Jack hid behind the van and waited. Nothing. Then, at the corner of the street he saw movement. Was it one of Hemple's men? Was it Ezra? Or Cliff?

It was neither. Round the corner came a small heavy-coated figure wrapped up to the eyes in scarves and with a strange fur cap. It was just a small boy – too small to be Harry or one of his bully friends, and much too small to be Cliff or Ezra. The boy darted along, hiding every few steps behind a tree or a lamp-post. As he came alongside the van, Jack darted out and grabbed him by the arm. The boy screamed, then went silent.

"Who are you?" growled Jack, searching to find the face of his snooping enemy.

"Please let go. Please." Jack released his grip, and the boy slowly unwound the scarf from his face. *His* face? No. It was a girl. A girl he recognized from somewhere.

"I've seen you before," said Jack. "What's your name?"

"Lucy," she murmured nervously.

"I remember you – you were with Harry and his friends that day in Mr. Hemple's back yard."

"Yes, I was."

"You're Lucy Hemple."

Lucy hesitated. "Yes," she said finally.

"And you were *specially* nasty to me."

"Yes, I was." She paused again. "But I'm sorry."

"Well…that's all right, I guess," said Jack with a smile. "At least you didn't hit me like the others!"

"I'm sorry," said Lucy again, looking up into Jack's piercing grey eyes.

"What are you doing following me around? Especially at this hour of the morning?"

"I've thought about you ever since that day. You looked like a nice person, and you were very brave. I wanted to see you again, but I didn't think I ever would because my whole family seems to hate you."

"Why, do you suppose?"

"Oh, it isn't really you. It's Mr. Howe they hate."

Jack looked at her sharply.

"Joe Howe?"

"Yes, Joe Howe." Lucy paused for a moment, and then the words came in a rush. "Father keeps saying that Mr. Howe is trying to start a revolution. He's been saying bad things in his paper about Father and the other magistrates for years, and now with this letter that he put in the paper last month they say they've had enough. They all met at our house last week, and talked about all sorts of ways of getting rid of him if the governor wouldn't have him arrested. Mr. Roach who runs the poorhouse said he wanted to challenge him to a duel because of the way he was slandered in that letter. They even talked of having him murdered one night in the street, or pistolled in his office – that's what they said. They talked of you too – said you were a spy for him – "

"How do you know all this?"

"I listened at the door. Tell me – is Mr. Howe really such a terrible man?"

"Mr. Howe? Mr. Howe is the most wonderful man who ever lived." Jack found himself with tears in his eyes as he said this: he meant it with all his heart.

"Then why would they hate him so?"

"Because he's brave enough to point out how crooked and corrupt your father…your father's friends are. Everyone in town hates those magistrates and the things they do. Their taxes are very unfair, they make big profits on the backs of the people, they keep all the power to themselves and never listen to anyone…" Jack could have gone on a long time – he knew the whole scandal inside out. But he stopped, and looked gently at little Lucy. "You don't want to hear all this."

"Yes, I do. And Jack? My father…" She hesitated. "My father is as bad as any of them."

"What do you mean?"

Lucy burst into tears. Jack put his arm around her, and comforted her. All of a sudden he heard a noise, and looking round he saw the baker stumping down the steps of the nearest house with a big baker's basket. Jack hushed Lucy and quickly pulled her towards some bushes on the other side of the street. But the baker heard them and stopped in his tracks.

"Hey you!" he shouted. They froze.

"What are you no-goods loitering around here for at this hour of the morning?" And he started menacingly across the alley towards them.

"Run," whispered Jack, taking Lucy's hand. "Run!"

They took off like stags down the icy lane. The baker began to follow them, but stumbled and fell, and gave up with a curse. He limped back angrily to his van, climbed onto the driving seat, whipped up his little horse and took off in the other direction.

Jack and Lucy stopped to catch their breath. "That was not just a baker," panted Jack.

"What do you mean?" asked Lucy, wide-eyed.

"I've seen him before. In…a place where smugglers were." Jack caught himself in time. He couldn't give too much away. But there was no doubt about it – the baker had been one of the two men coming up the stairs from the amazing smugglers' cellar he had peeked into on Christmas Day. He even remembered the name the other one had called him: "Pat."

"Let's go to the dockers' booth on the corner and get a glass of tea," said Jack. "I'm frozen – aren't you?"

"No, I must go home. If father knows I'm out of the house he'll punish me again." Lucy started to sob once more.

"Does he punish you often?"

"Yes, and Harry too. Almost every day."

"That's terrible," said Jack earnestly. "Is that what you meant when you said he was a bad man?"

"Not only that," said Lucy: "I think he's…I think he does bad things. Things they'd send him to jail for if they found out."

"Like smuggling?"

"How did you know?"

Jack hesitated. "I guessed."

"I think he's afraid your Joe Howe will find him out…It was

my father who said at that meeting that Joe Howe should be…murdered. And he said he has people who would do it…. There. Now I've told you."

"Thank you, Lucy. You're very brave."

"I must go now."

"Find out all you can. – And look, I go past your house almost every day. If you ever need help, put something red in the window. Or come to our office on Granville Street."

Lucy nodded. "My room's right above the front door. Bye-bye." She turned and scampered down the street, looking round to give one last wave.

As he waved back, Jack realized he was at least half an hour late for his next deliveries. He raced as fast as he could all the way back to the office.

"Where've you been, lad?" asked Mr. McNab, handing him his next bundle of papers, and looking at him fiercely from under his bushy black eyebrows.

"I . .er . . I met a friend."

"We don't pay you to play about. Get at it now, sharp!"

"Yessir." Jack took the scolding without a murmur, and skipped back out the door to make his next round.

CHAPTER ELEVEN

A VISITOR FOR MR. HOWE

For the next couple of days while he went about his work, Jack thought about his strange meeting with Lucy and what she had told him. Should he pass it on to Joe? Maybe not, because Joe would ban him again from going about the town, and the mere thought of that made him shudder. Besides, even if they were out to kill Joe, what could Joe do about it? The police themselves were all under the control of the magistrates – they'd be told not to lift a finger to defend him.

He had blurted out that warning to Joe the next morning, but wished he hadn't, and got out of the office quickly before he could be questioned any further. Perhaps it was warning enough, if Joe and Mrs. Howe took him seriously. Meanwhile, he would tell Rob and the other apprentices that he had heard the rumour. His chance came at the end of that day when they were all gathered in the backroom changing out of their printing aprons and clogs. The boys listened in amazement, but they had learned to respect this young lad who was so bright and quick, and every one of them swore to keep an eye out for any danger to their beloved master. Little did Joe know that his band of apprentices had become his bodyguards!

The very next day at the office – it was the fourth day of February and bitterly cold – the boys had just finished their morning session with Joe when there was a loud knock on the front door.

"Go and see who on earth that is, will you, Jack? It sounds like the rapping on the castle gate in *Macbeth*!"

Jack hurried to the door, and opened it to find a tall, portly man waiting on the doorstep. He was dressed in a long black cloak and carpet boots, and wore an official-looking black fur hat with a blue cockade stuck in at the side. Behind him, at a respectful distance, stood two policemen.

"Is Mr. Joseph Howe on the premises?" asked the fur hat.

"Yes, he is, sir," answered Jack. "Who shall I say is calling on him?"

"Mr. Button, from the attorney-general's office."

The attorney-general was the highest law officer in the country, and Jack took fright, dismayed by the stern look of the fur hat and by the policemen standing grimly beyond.

"Yes, sir," said Jack faintly. He ran in to Joe Howe and spluttered, "It's someone from the…the attorney-general's office…Mr. Button. With two policemen."

"Why, show them in at once!" cried Joe with a smile, putting down his pen and getting up from his chair. "It's a bitter day out there." Seeing Joe's calm, Jack got his courage again. He ran back to the door and said:

"Mr. Howe begs you all to step inside. This way please." Mr. Button turned to the policemen who were walking eagerly toward the door to escape from the cold and barked, "You wait out here." He followed Jack inside and into Joe Howe's office.

"Welcome, welcome, Mr. Button!" said Joe with a warm smile, his arms outstretched. "This is indeed a pleasure. Jack, get Mr. Button a glass of something to keep out the frost. What will you have, my friend?"

"I will not be staying long, Mr. Howe. I am here simply to give you this." He drew from his black cloak a large envelope with a red wax seal upon it, and handed it formally to Joe. "Attorney-General Archibald requested me to place it personally in your hands."

"Well, that's very good of him," said Joe genially, taking the envelope and turning it over. "Would you like me to read it while you are here?"

"Please yourself, Mr. Howe." Joe picked up a paper-knife and slit the envelope open, pulling out a single sheet of paper. He read it swiftly, and then looked up at Mr. Button.

"Is there anything else you need to tell me, Mr. Button?"

"No, Mr. Howe."

"Why then, thank you. Jack!…Mr. Dance will see you to the door. And a very good morning to you."

As soon as Jack had closed the door behind Mr. Button he returned to the office, and found Joe at the window looking out at his parting guest.

"Is it bad, sir?" ventured Jack.

Joe turned and looked directly at the young fellow he had come to love and trust.

"Oh, bad, good, I don't know, Jack. At least I haven't been murdered," he added with a smile. "Go home and ask Mrs. Howe to come by the office as soon as she can, will you?"

"Yes sir." He turned to go.

"Do you know what libel is, Jack?"

"Yes, sir, it's when you say something or write something nasty about someone else and they take you to court for it."

"That's right. That's right. Well, the attorney-general has written to tell me he intends to sue me for seditious libel against the magistrates of Halifax.'"

"Because of the letter?"

"Because of the letter, just so."

"But shouldn't Mr. Thompson be sued for writing it?"

"Mr. Thompson? Mr. Thompson? Who is he? The letter was signed by 'The People.'" Joe looked fixedly at Jack, who blushed and bit his lip.

"Yes, sir…Is it a serious crime, sir?"

"Yes, I'm afraid it is. Especially *seditious* libel, which implies that you are stirring people up against the king. If they find you guilty, you can be fined and put in prison for years."

"Oh, that's terrible."

"Now run along and fetch Mrs. Howe."

"Yes, sir."

"And then tell Mr. McNab I want to speak to the whole staff in about half an hour."

"Yes, sir." Jack was out of the door again like lightning and tore down the street.

Soon Mrs. Howe and the whole printshop had heard from Joe just what had happened. They were angry and fearful, but Joe raised their spirits by cracking jokes and making light of it all. At the end, though, he turned serious, and he said:

"Boys, friends, all of you – and Susan Ann, my dear wife – remember why we published that letter. This town is being run by the most neglectful and stupid men that ever mismanaged a people's affairs. Someone had to take the risk and speak out, and it is we – you and I. Don't you worry – whatever happens I'll be fine and dandy. But we're not just fighting to save Joe Howe from being fined and thrown into jail. We're fighting for the right to say freely what we think and what we feel about the way this beloved town of ours is being run. We are fighting for freedom – the freedom of the press. Isn't that worth fighting for?"

"Three cheers for Mr. Howe!" cried Mr. McNab. His loyal staff cheered him to the rafters, and Susan Ann embraced him in front of them all.

"Thank'ee, all of you, thank'ee. And now Mrs. Howe and I are going home to plan strategy and have a crust to eat while we are doing it! I'll be back this afternoon, and will be writing a column for tomorrow's paper. Be ready to strike it off, Mr. McNab!"

"I'll be waiting, sir."

"Good. Now boys: to work again!"

They laughed and filed back into the printshop. Once again, Jack couldn't help admiring the way Joe Howe handled the whole affair.

"Good. Now boys: to work again!"

He was rather a solemn boy, he decided, and there and then made a resolution that if he was in danger he would always look for the funny side of things. He could not have known at the time, but very soon he would have good cause to remember his resolution.

In the column he wrote that afternoon, Joe Howe told his readers quite openly of the warning notice he had received from the attorney-general, and of the threat of a prosecution against him. He was scornful of the magistrates, and said he was sure that even if they won their case they would do themselves great damage. By the next day, what he wrote was in the hands of hundreds of people in the town, and soon through the whole of Nova Scotia. In taverns, in clubs and stores, down on the wharves and out on the fishing-boats, in the coal mines of Stellarton and the gypsum quarries of Windsor, Nova Scotians talked of little else. Folks in important positions, like councillors and magistrates and army officers and their friends and families, were delighted that the villain Howe was finally going to be brought to justice. But for the majority of the people, especially in Halifax, it was a different story. They had suffered for years under these rascally men, and there had been endless complaints. Now at last someone was standing up to them.

Jack delivered his papers that morning faster than ever before, not even stopping for his occasional chats with the milkman or boys heading to school or servants walking their masters' dogs. There was a reason for hurrying so: he had passed Mr. Hemple's house with his papers just as it was growing light, and glancing up at the window above the front door, as he had promised to do, he saw there, right in the middle, a large, red Christmas candle. His heart missed a beat. Lucy was in trouble! As soon as he had thrown his last paper onto the last porch of the last house, he ran back down the hill to Mr. Hemple's. There it was, number 17. He came up to it cautiously, hiding behind a tree on the other side of the street. Yes, there in the middle window sat the red candle still. What now? He couldn't very well knock at the door and ask for Lucy.

Jack carefully scanned the front of the house. At the side of the porch below Lucy's window was a trellis, holding up some kind of fruit tree. If it was strong enough to bear his weight, maybe he could get to the porch roof and be right outside the window. Was Lucy in her room? He decided to try throwing a snowball against the glass, and bent down to pick up some snow in his mittens.

At that moment he heard the crunch of footsteps in the snow. He jumped behind the tree again, and looked out warily. Two men were coming down the street. Between them, held tightly on each side, was Lucy. Jack soon recognized the men. Mr. Hemple had Lucy in an armlock and was striding along with his head up and a cruel smile on his face. Cliff held her other arm and was limping along with his hand over Lucy's mouth to stop her screams: her feet were dragging along in the snow, and she was making the most piteous, muffled sounds. It was more than Jack could stand. With a bound he leapt out from behind the tree, pelted across the road and took a flying jump at Mr. Hemple, who lost his footing in the snow, let go of Lucy and sprawled into the snowbank with a howl of anger and pain. Jack fell over too but did a quick somersault and was up in a second. Cliff still had hold of Lucy and was dragging her as fast as he could to the door of the house when Jack came up from behind and tripped him. Cliff stumbled and Jack pulled Lucy out of his hands.

"Run, Lucy, run! You know where to go – run, for heaven's sake!"

For an agonising few seconds Lucy stood there, while her father dragged himself up and was about to lunge at her, with Jack ready to push him off again. At last she started away, and sped down the street and out of sight. Her father bellowed after her: "Lucy-y-y! Come back here you wretched girl! Lucy-y-y!"

Jack started to run too, but suddenly felt himself pinned from behind. Cliff had got to his feet and caught him in an iron grip.

"Bring that little brute inside!" said Mr. Hemple with a snarl. "I'll deal with him."

CHAPTER TWELVE

MRS. HOWE ON THE WARPATH

Young Rob Woollings was sweeping fresh snow from the doorstep of *The Novascotian*, when he looked up to see a small girl standing a few paces away. She was panting, sobbing and swaying from side to side. She wore no hat or gloves. Her coat was torn, and blood was oozing from a cut on her cheek.

"What's with you, little girl?" said Rob. He put down his broom and ran over to her, catching her just as she was about to fall. Lifting her up in his arms, he carried her gently inside. Joe Howe was out, so Rob took the girl into Joe's inner office, and laid her down in the armchair by the fire. She was still weeping, and Rob lent her his handkerchief, then ran to the washbasin in the printshop and brought a wet cloth to wash her wound. She took it from him and held it against her cheek.

"Thank you," she murmured, and slowly her sobs died down. Mr. McNab bustled in to put some proofs on Joe's desk.

"Who's this?" he said sharply, looking at the girl. Mr. McNab did not enjoy surprises, and this was certainly a surprise.

"I found her outside," said Rob nervously. "She nearly fainted."

"You did the right thing," said Mr. McNab gruffly, putting his proofs down. "Go fetch Mrs. Howe."

Rob hesitated, but Mr. McNab sounded firm, so away he trotted.

"What's your name, lass?" asked Mr. McNab.

"Lucy," she replied.

"In some kind of trouble?"

"Yes. But I escaped. Jack helped me. I think he's been taken away by my father."

Mr. McNab's bushy eyebrows jumped up and down.

"Jack? Jack Dance?"

"Yes, I think so."

"Who's your father?"

"Mr. Hemple."

"Magistrate Hemple?"

"Yes."

"Heaven help us. How do you know Hemple's got hold of him?"

"When I was running away I looked round, and saw Cliff holding him tight, and my father was hitting him in the face." She burst into tears again. Mr. McNab took no notice.

"Cliff?"

"Father's butler. And he does a lot of other things too. He's a very bad man."

"Where was this?"

"Outside our house. On Salter Street."

Joe's office door opened swiftly, and Susan Ann Howe swept in, her long skirts trailing, with Rob hovering behind.

"Oh my poor darling, what's happened to you?" She hurried over to Lucy and knelt beside her chair. She pushed back the girl's flaxen hair, examining her for other cuts and bruises. Her concern and gentle touch made Lucy cry even more.

"Who did this to you?"

Lucy's mouth tightened in a line and she didn't answer.

"From what she told me," said Mr. McNab, "it may have been her father, Magistrate Hemple. – Name's Lucy," he added as an afterthought.

Susan Ann looked back grimly at Mr. McNab, who went on: "And she says Hemple has gotten hold of Jack."

"What?" Susan Ann rose to her feet. Quickly Mr. McNab repeated what Lucy had told him.

"Where's Mr. Howe?" she asked abruptly.

"Seeing some legal fellow over the water in Dartmouth."

"Oh, yes, I remember."

"He won't be back till early evening."

Susan Ann thought for a few moments, then turned to Rob Woollings.

"Rob," she said, "Mr. McNab and I are going out for a while. I'm asking you to be in charge of the office."

"Yes, Ma'am," said Rob, a little awed by the responsibility he was being given.

"Tell Peter and Jim and Bill what has happened. Lock the outer door after us, and don't let in any strangers. Is that clear?"

Though Mr. McNab was Joe Howe's partner, and kept tight control of the printshop, he never questioned who should make decisions in Joe's absence. Susan Ann took command effortlessly, and her quick mind commanded respect.

"Rob, send Bill up to Jack's mother on William Alley. Tell her he's in some kind of trouble, and not to be alarmed. If he's not home at his usual time, I suggest she come down to the office here for more news. Do you go to school, Lucy?"

"No, ma'am. I have a governess who comes twice a week."

"How can your mother let you out on the street?"

"My mother's dead, ma'am."

"Oh, I'm sorry to hear that…Now Lucy, my dear, you will stay here with Rob and the other apprentices. Rob, look after her: get her something hot to drink. Show her round the printshop if she would like to see it. And if Mrs. Dance comes, make sure she's looked after too. Do you understand?"

"Yes, Ma'am," said Rob. "Come with me, Lucy. Come and see where we work."

"No idling now, Woollings," said Mr. McNab. "There's a lot of new business advertisements to set up. I'll want them done by this evening."

"Yes, sir."

"You'll need your warm things, Mr. McNab."

"Yes, Mrs. Howe."

<hr/>

Five minutes later, Mr. McNab and Mrs. Howe were walking briskly south along Granville Street. Mrs. Howe had picked up Joe's old umbrella from the stand in the hall. Mr. McNab carried his cane. They were an odd couple: Mr. McNab was as thin as a bird and walked like one. Susan Ann Howe flowed along the street like a sailing ship in full rig. But they were alike in their determination. "I hope we're in time," said Mrs. Howe. "People have a reputation for disappearing when they get in Hemple's way. And Jack's had brushes with him before."

∞

Josiah Hemple had come to Halifax from the Boston States as a young man, with nothing but the clothes he stood up in. But he soon made his way in the little world of Halifax. He got his first job as a merchant's clerk down in one of the huge fish-stores on the wharf, big as churches, where fishermen brought their catches from up and down the shore to be salted and cured before being packed up in barrels and shipped to the West Indies.

Through his work in the office Hemple came to know the whole tribe of merchants up and down the docks, and as he rose in the business, he took ship several times to Jamaica and Trinidad, where he got friendly with the British colonists that were settled there. They were making fortunes by exporting rum, sugar and molasses from their sugar plantations, which were worked by slaves. Josiah soon realized that there was a fortune to be made by importing these goods into Nova Scotia without paying heavy taxes.

He saw another opening too. Since the American Revolution, Britain had forbidden its merchants to trade with America, and refused to let American ships into British ports, including the ports of colonies like Nova Scotia. So there were also great opportunities for smuggling goods secretly from America, and selling them on the black market.

Hemple set up business, and soon made a name for himself as the respectable import and export firm of "Josiah Hemple, Merchant." Behind this respectable front he slowly built up a vast smuggling network of sea captains, sailors, dockhands, brokers, stage coach drivers, porters and warehouse owners – some of the shadiest people in Halifax. Hemple kept away from this rabble: they were organised by his right-hand man, Matt Frygood, the shrewd, ruthless old soak that Jack had caught sight of as master of the Christmas feast in the smugglers' cellar.

As a rising young merchant, Hemple had gradually become accepted by the powerful people of Halifax. He married the daughter of a British garrison officer, and they became regular and welcome guests at Government House. His wife died giving birth to Lucy, but Hemple was by that time well in with the powerful men who ran the province, so it was not long before he was invited to become one of the magistrates appointed by the governor to run the town and county of Halifax. He had accepted happily, seeing it not only as an honour but as yet another opportunity for making money.

In recent years, though, his fortunes had taken a dive. There were three reasons for this. First, the British had made it easier to trade with the United States, so his smuggling operations in America were much less profitable. Second, the British abolished slavery, which meant the sugar plantations had to pay their workers; this caused the price of rum to go up, which cut into Hemple's profits. Third – and most seriously – Joseph Howe's newspaper, *The Novascotian*, had started speaking up about some of the things going on in the town, which meant that crooked dealings like smuggling were becoming more and more risky. Josiah Hemple was afraid of losing not only his illegal profits but also his place in the smart society of Halifax. If only he could silence that man Howe!

∾

Under these pressures, Josiah Hemple had become angry and bitter, and more and more dangerous. His children lived in fear of him. Harry tried to survive by doing everything he could to copy his father, desperate to please and impress him. But Lucy was a rebel. That morning he had whipped her for not eating her breakfast, and sent her to her room. She had put her Christmas candle in the window, but then decided to try and find Jack, to get away however she could. She crept down to the hall and was putting on her coat and boots when she heard someone approaching from the kitchen. She quickly opened the back door and stumbled down the steps into the garden.

"Hey! Lucy, come back here at once you little devil!" It was Cliff. She didn't even turn round but scampered into the bushes at the foot of the yard and scrambled over the same wall that Jack had jumped weeks before. Cliff alerted Mr. Hemple, and it wasn't long before they caught her wandering near the harbour, and marched her back to Salter Street. With Jack's help, she had made her escape, but now Jack himself was in the clutches of this ruthless man.

Mr. Hemple was striding back and forth in his study. He was red with rage. "Clifford!" he bellowed at last.

"Yes, sir?"

"Come in here."

Cliff entered Mr. Hemple's study, and found his master standing, like an old tiger, in front of the window.

"Shut the door. Come on – quick about it! We don't have much time."

Cliff's thin lips tightened as he turned and closed the door behind him. He was still breathing heavily from all that had happened, and his bad leg was giving him pain.

"Where is he?"

"Safe, sir."

"Safe *where*, yer fool?"

"In the coal-hole." The coal-hole was a small room in the basement of the house. Coal for the stoves and fires of Mr. Hemple's house was delivered every few weeks, shovelled down a shute from the outside. It was a dismal, unheated place, thick with coal dust.

"Is he conscious?"

"I think so, sir. But you hit him a nasty punch."

"Never yer mind about that. Now listen – "

"I've sent a message to Matt, sir. He'll be sending up a couple of men and a wagon to take him down the street to the cellar. They'll be here in a few minutes. We'll get him on board *Saucy Jane* as soon as she docks, and then – " Cliff drew his thumbnail across his throat and gestured "overboard."

"Y're even more of a fool than I thought," blazed Mr. Hemple, looking at his servant with disgust. "Don't yer realize this little critter's worth a gold mine to us while he's alive?"

Cliff looked at him.

"I don't understand."

"Harry tells me he's so far in with that pot-stirrer Joseph Howe he's like another son to him. Put the boy under a fear of having his throat cut if yer will, but then make sure Howe knows about it and we'll have him in the palm of our hands. No more sniffin' around lookin' for trouble. No more slimy hints in that paper of his. We'll have him shut up even before the courts get him put away in that libel case."

"Will he lose the case, d'you reckon, sir?"

"Sure as eggs are eggs. Not a leg to stand on."

The door bell clanged.

"That'll be yer men. What are they doin' at the front door, the idiots? Send them to the side entrance, and get the little brute out of here. Quick now."

Cliff couldn't help letting out a sigh as he left the study. Mr. Hemple had become a hard man to work for. He limped to the front door and opened it.

"This is Mr. Hemple's house, I believe?"

He had not seen this smartly dressed woman before, nor the thin, dark-haired gentleman standing beside her in a tall hat.

"Er, yes. Yes it is, ma'am." Cliff was still recovering from his surprise at not seeing Matt's men from the cellar.

"Is he at home?"

"Er…yes, he is, ma'am."

"We would like to have a word with him. It's an urgent matter."

"Yes, ma'am. Please come in. Who shall I say is calling?"

"This is Mr. McNab." Cliff nodded at him. "And I am Mrs. Joseph Howe." She smiled charmingly at him. Cliff froze. Mr. Hemple would never forgive him. But it was too late. They were walking past him into the hall. Cliff closed the front door and crossed the hall to the study. He knocked and entered, shutting the door behind him.

"Quite a place," said Mr. McNab, eyeing the tall ceiling and the rich furnishings while they waited.

"Ill-gotten gains," murmured Susan Ann softly. But she was looking around for a different reason. Was Jack here?

"Why, Mrs. Howe! This is an honour indeed! Please step into the drawing-room...Mr. McNab? A pleasure!" Mr. Hemple was all smiles as he shook hands with both his visitors and led the way across the hall. Cliff bowed, then hurried out through the front door again, just in time to see a baker's wagon pulling up in front.

"Yer were lucky to find me in, good people," said their host, careful to close the drawing-room door behind them: "Pray sit down."

"I'll think I'll stand, thank you, Mr. Hemple. We are here because we have reason to believe that a boy called Jack Dance is somewhere in your house. We have come to collect him."

"Jack Dance? Jack Dance? 'Fraid I don't even know the name."

"You may remember him coming into your back garden around Christmastime looking for his toboggan – which you had burnt." Susan Ann smiled sweetly at him.

"Oh, was that...?"

"And he was seen outside this very house less than an hour ago. With you."

"With me?"

"You were hitting him." She looked straight at him, and Mr. Hemple began looking defiantly back at her. But he was no match for those keen blue eyes. He turned his head away and shifted towards the window. Looking out into the street, he just caught sight of the back end of a wagon drawn up outside the tradesman's entrance.

"Oh, that young man..."

"Yes, that young man. Where is he?"

"I did give him a bit of a clip – he was annoying my daughter, and I won't have that kind of thing. But then he took off down the street. Quick as lightning. 'Fraid I have no idea where he was headed."

"Are you sure?"

Mr. Hemple turned. "Mrs. Howe, I'm surprised you should

question the word of a magistrate."

"I'm surprised that you're surprised, Mr. Hemple. As you know, my husband's newspaper seems to have uncovered several examples of magistrates being loose with the truth."

"It's the kind of thing we at *The Novascotian* are pretty good at winkling out, as you know," put in Mr. McNab.

"Your newspaper is doing no service to the people of Nova Scotia by causin' them to lose trust in their government," shot back Mr. Hemple. "Mr Howe is givin' great distress to the lieutenant-governor and his council, as well as to the magistrates. If he's not careful he'll find his promisin' career brought to an abrupt end." By this time the polite mask had slipped off. His jaw was working, and his eyes rolled furiously at his visitors, but with great effort he got control of his temper, and smiled again. He had to keep them in the house at all costs – until the wagon had left with its burden. He could already hear sounds of muffled footsteps in the basement below. He could see that Susan Ann had heard them too: she was listening intently, her face toward the floor.

"Well, it sounds as though luncheon is on its way," he said with a weak laugh. "That must be our cook gettin' potatoes from the root cellar. Can I interest my guests in somethin' to eat?"

"I don't think we need food," replied Susan Ann, glancing over at Mr. McNab: "But I've been admiring your splendid house and its furniture. Would you be good enough to let us see some of your treasures?" And before he could reply she moved rapidly towards the door. Mr. McNab followed close behind.

"Oh, I'm afraid I need a little more warnin' for that kind of thing," he said, moving hastily to try and block them from leaving the room. "I'm a widower, yer know. The place is not as tidy as it should be. Mrs. Howe? One moment please…"

But Susan Ann had already darted out into the hall. Dropping all pretence at politeness she opened one door after another, with Mr. McNab holding Mr. Hemple at bay with his cane.

"Mrs. Howe, this is extremely rude of you. I must ask you to leave my house this moment."

She took no notice, and was starting up the big staircase to the second floor when they all heard the bang of a door closing. It came from the kitchen. She turned on her heel, and ran toward the kitchen door, pushing it open as she went.

At a table in the middle of the room an old maidservant was peeling potatoes. At a counter in the corner, Cliff was quietly polishing silver and humming to himself. They both looked up in surprise.

"Oh, I'm so sorry," she said, retreating. "I thought…" She closed the door again, and turned back into the hall to find Mr. Hemple right behind her.

"Ma'am," he snarled, "I will trouble yer to leave my house at once, or I will call the police. I've never been so insulted in my life. Get out, sir!" he shouted, wheeling round on Mr. McNab, who had raised his cane, ready to protect Mrs. Howe if Mr. Hemple raised a hand against her.

There was nothing to be done, and the two unwelcome visitors strode out with as much dignity as they could gather up. The door slammed behind them, and they walked out into the street, empty but for a solitary baker's horse and cart trotting away into the distance. They started back in silence.

"Did you believe his story that Jack ran away down the street?" asked Susan Ann at length.

"Not for a moment," said Mr. McNab, biting his lip in annoyance.

"Then is he in the house?"

"He certainly *was* in the house. But I guess Hemple would want to get him out of there as soon as possible. He doesn't like mixing his dirty doings with his lah-di-dah life as a magistrate."

"Then where would they have taken him?" she asked, with a catch in her voice.

"We shall see, won't we," said Mr. McNab grimly, as they turned the corner.

CHAPTER THIRTEEN

SURPRISES AND ESCAPES

It was dark when Joe Howe got back from Dartmouth. He had had a discouraging talk with John Prince, an old lawyer friend of his father's. Sedition, Mr. Prince told him, was a difficult charge to get out of, and he couldn't see any way that he, or any other lawyer for that matter, could help Joe fight the indictment. He advised Joe to apologize and withdraw the accusations, or almost certainly risk jail and a hefty fine.

"There's no way I am going to withdraw," said Joe quietly, but firmly. "It's not just for me, it's for the whole community. These things can't go on any longer." The old lawyer shook his grey head. But he lent Joe a couple of learned legal books, and suggested the names of other lawyers he could see. It was the best he could do, he said.

∾

The crossing back was rough and slow. The odd-shaped new steamboat ferry, with its black smoke-stack sticking up into the air like a pencil, first made its way carefully through slabs of pack ice floating along the shore, then had to chug across the harbour in the face of a sharp wind that had blown up from the south. They arrived late at the market slip, and with a cheery wave to the captain, Joe picked up his carpet-bag – loaded down with the heavy law books – and stepped down the gangway.

To his surprise he found Susan Ann waiting for him on the wharf, muffled up against the biting wind. Joe sensed at once that something was wrong.

"What is it, dear?" he asked, putting his arm round her shoulder. "Why are you here? You must be frozen."

"Oh Joe! Jack has been taken off by Hemple and his gang."

"Great heavens! Has that silly boy been up to his old tricks again?"

"I don't think it was his fault this time," she began, and while they made their way up the steep, sparsely lit street away from the harbour she described what had happened.

"He saw Lucy was being hurt, and came to her rescue. You would have done just the same, you know you would."

Joe nodded. Susan Ann went on to tell him of their fruitless visit to Mr. Hemple's house, and how she and Mr. McNab were almost sure he had been taken somewhere else, but they had no idea where.

"I can guess where. There are only two places: Hemple's warehouse on George Street, which his man Ezra runs, or Matt Frygood's cellar below the warehouse – the one that Jack stumbled into at Christmas. Where's Angus McNab now?"

"He's waiting at the office, with all the apprentices. How did it go with John Prince, by the way?"

"Not well. He thinks I should apologize and withdraw the accusations."

"Well, maybe we should think of that."

"I won't do it, dear. I'd rather be cast into prison for years than let those devils get away with their mischief. But let's think about Jack first. Have you told his mother what happened?"

"She's waiting at our house, and looking after Lucy, who refuses to go back to her father."

"What a mess. Now look, my dear, we're nearly home now. You go in to warm up by the fire and be with them. I'll head on to the office and plan a strategy with Angus and the boys."

"Don't do anything dangerous, Joe, I beg you."

"I can't promise that, dear. They're dangerous men."

With a quick kiss they parted at the front door of the house. Susan Ann's eyes followed Joe anxiously as he went on down the street with his usual carefree stride.

Jim had assembled the four apprentices in the hallway to wait for Joe's return. They stood there awkwardly, caps in hand.

"Good evening, sir," they all said in chorus as Mr. McNab unbolted the front door and let Joe in.

"Hello boys! So what's this – Mr. McNab's private army?"

They laughed, happy that their leader was back among them. "So: we have a problem on our hands. Mrs. Howe tells me you've been very helpful all day. I thank you very much. Now why not go into the printshop and get back to work? Newspapers still have to come out, you know. Mr. McNab, we must talk: come into my office if you will."

"Yes, sir. We won't be alone, as you'll see, sir." Joe went to step into his familiar den, but stopped at the doorway in amazement.

"Well, good gracious me! What are you all doing here?" A crowd of men stood almost shoulder to shoulder in the small office. Some of them carried stout sticks and clubs; one was even holding a sword. Lit by the blazing fire and by the oil lamps hanging overhead, they looked a fierce bunch. But looking round them, Joe recognized them all as his good friends: Dr. Gregor was there, his old neighbour Bob Lawson, and the author of that troublesome letter, George Thompson. George came forward and shook Joe by the hand.

"Joe, we're glad you're back. We all got a message from McNab this afternoon to say that your printer's boy has been kidnapped by the Hemple gang. We decided to meet together here and wait for you."

Bob Lawson spoke up: "We've been talking…We all know what Josiah Hemple has been up to these many years, and maybe this is the moment when his whole rotten business can be exposed for what it is. But we're afraid for you, Joe." He looked around at the others. George broke in:

"You're already in deep trouble with the magistrates, and with the governor and his council that run this whole benighted country. If you go after Hemple now you won't have a shred of support behind you. You won't have the police because they report to the magistrates. You won't have the army because they report to Governor Campbell. So as you see, we've all come prepared to do battle…" He looked round at the others and they raised their weapons with a grim smile. "And I've even brought you a pair of pistols, Joe, because I was pretty sure you didn't have any of your own." As he spoke, he placed a box of polished oak on the desk, opened it up and displayed two sleek pistols lying in a bed of blue velvet, their steel glinting in the firelight.

Joe looked round the room. These were his friends. They cared for him, and everything they were saying was for his benefit. All eyes were on him, and his gaze went from face to face to face. There was silence for a few moments. Then he spoke:

"Gentlemen…friends: I very much appreciate your concern for me. And I know that this libel case is not just about me but about the future of our whole community, and that it mustn't go wrong. We have a chance − a slim chance, I was told today by a lawyer friend, but a chance just the same − to put an end to a corrupt and slovenly system of town government, which is weighing us all down with unjust taxes, crooked police, bribery, and profiteering. Nothing should get in the way of that…Nothing…except the duty to do what is right and what is just at this very moment." He strolled over to the desk and picked up one of the pistols, weighing it in his hand.

"A few weeks ago a young fool of my acquaintance threatened to challenge me to a duel."

There was a murmur of surprise.

"If he does," he went on, "I shall have to accept the challenge, or be accused for the rest of my life of being a coward. So, George, I may well need to borrow these from you in the future, in self-defence. But you must know, my friends, that I never want the blood of any man on my hands." Watched intently by his friends, he calmly returned the pistol to its box and closed the lid.

"So wave your weapons around if you wish − there are times when discretion is not the better part of valour. But I have always thought of myself as a man of peace, and I want to stay that way. My boy has been kidnapped and his life is in danger. But meeting violence with violence makes us nothing but murderers too.

An attack on Hemple's house would be foolhardy, surely you can see that – many of us might be hurt, and I would certainly be an easy target for his bunch of cronies. But there is another way. It's nearly midnight, I know, but I am going straight to Government House, and will demand an immediate audience with His Honour. He is a man of integrity, and I am confident that he will listen, and that he will act."

Joe's friends looked at him. This was a Joe they had not seen or heard before. His thrilling voice, and his moral intensity, had a powerful effect on them. They looked at Joe's strong features, his pale face gleaming with perspiration in that hot and crowded room, his eyes bright with honesty and determination. Several of them said afterwards that they sensed at that very moment for the first time that this was not just a good newspaper man, a cheery friend and a devoted father and husband, but that there was greatness in him. That if fate was with him, he would do something to make the larger world a better place. They suddenly felt embarrassed by their assortment of sticks and swords and muskets – like schoolboys on a spree.

"Will you drop your weapons and come with me?"

There was a murmur among the men. It took Joe's courage and faith to think of going straight to the highest power in the land. They began to stack their sticks in the corner of the office.

"I reckon we're with you, Joe," said one.

Just then, there was a hammering at the outside door of *The Novascotian*. Mr. McNab went to see who was making the din. The men could hear the bolts being drawn back, the door opening, and a muffled exclamation. A moment later Mr. McNab re-entered the room with a bemused look on his face.

"A gentleman to see you, sir."

He stood back and in walked…Jack Dance! A cheer went up. Joe looked hard at the boy, shaking his head in wonder but smiling with pleasure and relief. Rob and the other apprentices had run into the hall when they heard the noise at the door, and now crowded in behind Jack, cheering and clapping.

"Well, my Jack," said Joe, going over to him and putting his arms round him. "You scamp! What in heaven's name has been happening? Let's look at you first."

Jack had a great red welt across the side of his head, his hair was filled with bits of straw, his face and hands and clothes were black, and he wore only one boot. He was panting, and his teeth were chattering with cold. But the look on his face was radiant. As he looked round at the crowd of grown men he was actually laughing – a mischievous devil of a laugh that soon had everyone in the room laughing along without knowing why.

"Get him to the fire," said George. "The boy's cold."

"Just a minute," said Jack, still chuckling. "There's someone with me. Where are you Will?" He walked back into the hall, and returned, pulling by the hand a middle-aged black man dressed in rags and with bare feet. He had a steel bracelet round one ankle, with a length of chain attached to it, which he was dragging over the floor behind him.

"This is Will, everybody," said Jack. "He saved my life."

If Jack was cold, poor Will was frozen solid. He was shaking all over, swaying from side to side and moaning. He seemed not even to know where he was. Joe took him by the arm and half carried him over to the fire, sitting him down in the armchair. Dr. Gregor went to Will and put his frozen feet between his hands, first one, then the other, and checked for signs of frostbite. Joe turned to the door.

"Rob," he cried. "Fetch some hot drinks for these fellows! And Mike, run back to my house and fetch Jack's mother and Mrs. Howe. Jack, you must have a story to tell. When the ladies arrive, will you tell it to us?" Jack nodded.

There was a bustling and busy-ness as hot drinks and apples and hunks of bread were fetched. When the two ladies arrived, eyes shining with tears, Jack ran into his mother's arms and they kissed and hugged, making everyone else a little tearful too. Then he gave Mrs. Howe a kiss and a hug, and shook Mr. McNab's hand and the hands of all the apprentices, who lined up like players at the end of a game of hurley. The need for Joe's friends to be there had vanished with the arrival of Jack and Will, but not one of them moved. They all wanted to hear Jack's story, and were chattering and laughing as they waited for the telling to begin. Joe had found a bottle of rum in his cupboard, and handed out little shots of the fiery liquid to everyone who wanted it. Dr. Gregor prescribed a tablespoon of it for Will, who coughed and spluttered as it went down, then, for the first time, smiled and even chuckled. As Joe said afterwards, it was quite a party.

Chairs were found for Mrs. Dance and Susan Ann, and everyone else sat or stood or perched on stools or on the arms of chairs. It had become so hot with all the people that, in spite of the cold outside, Mr. McNab got Peter the apprentice to open the window a crack.

Finally everyone settled down, and Joe turned to Jack.

"Well, my boy, are you warmed up enough to tell us your tale? What on earth have you been doing? And how in God's name did you get away?"

"Start from when Mr. Hemple hit you over the face," called out Susan Ann. "I can see it was a nasty blow."

"Well, I think it knocked me out. I – "

"Can't hear, Jack. Speak up!" cried out someone from the back of the room.

"Can't even see the boy!" shouted another.

Joe picked up the boy in his arms and stood him on top of the desk.

"There you are, Jack!" said Joe with a smile, steadying him with a hand in case he fell. "You're on stage! Fire away!"

And Jack, with a calm quite beyond his years, began to speak.

CHAPTER FOURTEEN

JACK TELLS HIS STORY

"When I helped Lucy get away," began Jack, "I think Mr. Hemple knocked me out. Where is Lucy by the way?" Jack interrupted himself, looking over to Susan Ann.

"Tucked up in bed at home and fast asleep. She's quite safe," Susan Ann assured him.

"Oh good. I did something right, anyway!" said Jack relieved, and there was a laugh. Then he went on with his account.

"When I woke up I was in a basement somewhere with a lot of coal and really black. They had stuffed a sock or something into my mouth and tied it behind, and they had tied my hands and my feet. I couldn't move except to roll around like…like a kind of worm." His audience chuckled, admiring Jack's way with words.

"I felt like crying. But then I remembered how Mr. Howe always cracks jokes when things are bad, and how it seems to make things better. So I started to laugh, except it's hard to laugh with a sock in your mouth." The audience tittered again.

"Really, I wasn't so upset about being in danger. I just felt I had let down Mr. Howe. He warned me not to get involved with Mr. Hemple again, and here I was right in his hands. I knew it would worry Mr. Howe just when he had his own dangers to worry about. I'm sorry, sir," he said ruefully, turning to Joe.

"So you should be, you silly idiot," replied Joe, "But since you were rescuing a damsel in distress, I can't very well blame you, can I?" There was laughter again. "Now get on with your story. What happened next?"

"My eyes were getting used to the darkness, and I was just

beginning to look around for something sharp to help me cut the rope on my hands, when the little trapdoor at the end of the hole opened, and a man crawled in. I couldn't move, of course, so he grabbed me easily and pulled me back to the trapdoor, where someone else took hold of me. I tried to kick him, and I think he hit me, because the next thing I knew I was in a cart of some kind, and one of the men was holding me down with my face on the floor, and we were going along a street and then we turned and went downhill for a while and then stopped. Then I think they rolled me inside a blanket, and carried me out of the cart, through a door and down some steps. And all of a sudden I knew where I was, because I knew that smell. I was in the smuggler's cellar – you know, Mr. Howe, the place I told you about at Christmas…"

"That's right, Jack, you did, and I guessed that's where they'd take you. So did you meet the loveable Matt Frygood?"

"Is that the man with a red face who wears a wig and drinks like a fish?" They laughed again.

"That's the one," said Joe with a smile.

"Yes I did. The moment they rolled me on to the floor out of the blanket there he was looking down at me with a very nasty look on his face. He had a jug of ale in his hand and he prodded me with his cane. And now I could see the faces of the men who had brought me there. One was Pat something-or-other, and the other was Silver from Hemple's warehouse.

"'Call Will from out back and tell him to throw this pile of dirt into the slave-hole,' said Mr. Frygood.

"Then Pat answered: 'Cliff said Hemple wants him on board *Saucy Jane* and out of the way quick.'

"'Do what I damn well say,' Frygood said. 'Hemple doesn't know what he is talking about – *Saucy Jane* won't be in till the turn of the tide.' He turned and shouted 'Will!' at the top of his voice, and Will – this Will," said Jack, indicating his friend by the fire, "he came running and picked me up and took me past all those amazing things they smuggle, and into a kind of cage, which he locked me into. Then he just walked away and I was left on the stone floor. It was very cold."

"I had to do it," piped up Will suddenly from the corner. "He'd have whipped me else. Always a-whippin' me, that one. He's a beast, that one."

"I don't know how long I was there," continued Jack, after taking a swig of the hot cocoa Rob had brought him, "but then I heard the sound of someone using a broom, and I looked out and saw Will sweeping the floor quite near the cage where I was. He got closer and closer, looking around all the time, then he came sweeping right up to the door, and without looking at me he said 'Listen, boy. Listen here and listen well. Here's a knife so you can cut yourself free. But do it so they can't see that you're free, understand me?'

"I told him I understood. Then he said: 'I'm going to help you escape, understand me? Small boy like you shouldn't be getting kicked around by these bad folks.' That's what he said."

"Yeah, that's what I said all right. 'Them's bad folks,'" said Will, laughing crazily. "People who say there's no more slaves in these parts don't know what they're talkin' 'bout. I'm a slave to that Frygood. Locks me in every night and chains me. Look!" And he raised his leg and showed the bracelet and its dragging chain. "But I fooled them! I fooled them good!" And he laughed his crazy laugh again.

"So I took the knife from the floor and started cutting the rope off my wrists. It was hard because they were tied behind me. It took me ages – I don't know how long. Then I tied it very loosely again, and hid the knife in my boot.

"I heard everything getting very quiet in the cellar, and all the lamps seemed to go out. And then, I heard a door open and footsteps coming closer. I lay down on the floor as though I couldn't move. I could see the shadows of two men with a lantern, and I saw Will with them. He unlocked the door of the cage, and they came in and picked me up. I pretended to be asleep. They put me in a sack and I felt myself being lifted on to a man's shoulder and he walked away. They didn't say anything.

"I heard a door open and could feel we were outside. I was very frightened, and all I could think of was that Will had said he would help me escape, and I knew he was there – I heard one tell him to shut the door behind them and go along.

"Soon I could hear the waves against the wharf so I knew we were at the harbour. Then the man went down some steps and I felt him step into a little rowboat. I was put down in the bottom of the boat. Then one of the men said 'Cast off, slavey, and take these oars. Look sharp!'"

"Yeh, that's what he said," butted in Will, "and of course I had to take them oars and do some rowin'!"

"Go on, boy, we're all listening!" said Joe, smiling almost proudly at Jack, and taking a sip of his rum and water.

"I could hear the sound of the oars in the water. I knew it must be dark, so I slipped the rope off my wrists and my feet. I guessed we might be going out to a ship in the harbour, but then I was wondering whether they might just throw me overboard. I can swim, but it was so cold I was sure I would never get back to shore. Mother, I started thinking of you."

Everyone looked over at Mrs. Dance, who burst into tears, and Jack jumped down from the desk and went to embrace her and dried her eyes with her handkerchief. She hugged him tight and kissed him. Then he went on with his story still holding her and sitting on the arm of her chair.

"Anyway, suddenly I felt the boat rock from side to side," continued Jack, "and I heard a shout and a big splash. Then there was a kind of thump and a scuffle, then another big splash and the sound of men crying out and splashing about. The boat kept rocking – but then that stopped and I heard the rowing again, much faster this time. And I heard Will say 'Come on, boy, quick! Get out of that there sack! Look alive now! Those devils'll be after us!'

"They hadn't tied the sack so I managed to crawl out of it. Then I saw we were right up against the wharf steps. 'Jump, boy!' said Will."

"'Jump', I said!'" came from Will by the fire, laughing again: "'Jump, jump, jump!'"

"And I jumped out of the rowboat, and Will jumped out too and we just left the boat there, and Will took me by the hand and we ran up the steps and Will wanted to run off down the wharf, but I said no – and *I* pulled *him* by the hand, and we ran all the way up the hill to here without stopping! And here we are!"

There was a laugh from everyone in the room, and a cheer, then someone started to clap, and they all clapped. And one or two of the men went over to Will and shook his hand. There was relief and happiness all round, and loud chatter and more laughs. Soon Joe called for silence.

"Good friends, it's a fine thing to hear a story with a happy ending. And you told it very well, Jumping Jack. You'll be a preacher one day, or a politician, I'm not sure which!" The room laughed again and someone called out "Hear, hear!"

"But, friends," he went on, "Let's not forget, that these two fellows, brave and resourceful as they were, were also very lucky. We have in this town a small but highly dangerous criminal set. There's no question Hemple and Frygood are running a criminal organization, and they are prepared to kill to defend it. To get our young Jack out of their clutches I was prepared to make big trouble. But now that he's safe, thanks to our friend Will here, this is not the time to confront them.

"Mrs. Dance, it's coming towards midnight. You and Jack will stay with us tonight – your old rooms are there waiting for you." Jack smiled at his mother and they clutched hands.

"What do we do with Lucy, Joseph?" asked Susan Ann, looking up at him anxiously.

"I have a feeling that that situation will sort itself out. For the moment let's just be sure she's looked after and given some love and tenderness. She needs that, and no one can give it better than you, my dear.

"And now I believe it's time we broke up this happy party and went home to bed. I for one have a lot on my plate. I shall be

visiting one or two more lawyers in the next few days – including you, Charles – to see what advice I can get about this libel suit. But one thing you may be sure of – I won't be backing down. I love this town, and come what will, while I have my health and my strength, I'll fight its enemies. Thank you for your help and your support. I shall need more of that in the days to come. God bless you all."

And so this strange party broke up. Joe's friends said their goodbyes to him and to Susan Ann and Mrs. Dance, and shook Jack's hand as they left. Mr. McNab got the apprentices to make Will a warm bed in the lunchroom at the back of the shop, and made sure the offices were locked and bolted. Then Jack, with a stout bodyguard of Joe, Susan Ann and his mother, made his way down the street to the loved and familiar home of the Howes. It was the end of a long and amazing day – as Jack used to say quietly afterwards: "I think this was the best adventure of all."

CHAPTER FIFTEEN

MR. HEMPLE LOOKS FOR LUCY

The next day dawned cold again but sunny and bright, the sky washed clean by the stiff night winds. Halifax folk were used to their Februaries being dark and wretched, so they were out and about in good spirits. The following wind from the south had brought several ships to port ahead of schedule, and there was a heap of bustle down on the wharves, with cargoes being unloaded, customs officers checking goods, peddlers strapping huge crates to their backs for delivery to the stores, and army detachments collecting new supplies.

After the excitements of the day before, life at the office of *The Novascotian* was returning more or less to normal. Joe Howe had given Jack a few days off to recover from his ordeal and to be with his mother, and they would be walking home after breakfast. But he himself was at his desk before seven, covering page after page in his vigorous, flowing hand. Out in the printshop Angus McNab was tut-tutting over the apprentices' careless typesetting from the previous day. "No concentration," he muttered to himself, though he had to admit that there had been plenty of distractions. He had already had one himself today: Will had been waiting at the door an hour earlier when he opened up, and was about to dash out into the street and away.

"Now where would you be going, Will?" asked Angus.

It was clear that Will didn't know – that he was heading somewhere away from town, terrified above all of meeting Matt Frygood and being hauled back to the cellar and whipped and starved once again, or even killed. Angus found him a padded coat and a cap, and some old boots that had been left behind by an apprentice long gone. He gave him a couple of coins, and told him of a church up Brunswick Street where many black families were members of the congregation. And he told him to come back to Mr. Howe if he ever needed anything:

"Mr. Howe is uncommonly grateful to you, Will, for what you did for young Jack. We all are. You'll always have friends here. Fare ye well, then − and mind you keep away from the harbour!"

So off went Will, into a town where white folks still barely tolerated black folks, and then only as servants, or as poor peddlers trudging in from the country to sell brooms and wooden pails. There had been black families in the province ever since the American Revolution, when they had escaped from slavery to a free country. But there was a long way to go before these Nova Scotians found respect. As Angus closed the door he wondered whether the poor fellow would be better off than before. Being free was one thing − being happy was another. He shook his head sadly as he returned to his work.

Later in the morning Joe Howe planned on stepping out to make a call on another lawyer, asking again for advice on the prosecution. But producing a newspaper once a week was still his first task, and since he wrote most of it himself there was no business important enough to take him away from his pen and ink for long. One thing, however, he had attended to: he had sent Peter off to Salter Street with a message, addressed to His Worship Josiah Hemple, inviting him to drop by the offices of *The Novascotian* at his convenience. He enjoyed imagining Mr. Hemple's face when he read the note. Normally, the man would never have dreamed of seeking out the company of someone he so despised and feared. But Joe had a strong card in his hand…

❧

The Citadel clock struck nine. Joe had just completed a long article on the importance of Nova Scotia developing its arts and sciences as well as its trade and commerce. As he read it through before passing it on to Mr. McNab, the big iron knocker on the front door sounded through the building.

Mr. McNab sent Peter to find out who the caller was, and a minute or two later there came a knock at Joe's office door.

"Come in, come in," called Joe. The door burst open and the visitor strode in. Yes, Josiah Hemple, magistrate of Halifax and smuggler *extraordinaire*, was standing there and taking off his hat, in the office of his arch-enemy Joseph Howe.

Mr. Hemple looked as though he had not slept. He was unshaven, his hair was an unruly mess, and his shirt was open at the neck. His hands trembled, his eyes were bloodshot and his lips were pressed together in a thin line.

"Mr. Howe," he began in a shaking voice: " Mr. Howe…where – is – my – daughter?"

"Ah…you mean Lucy?"

"Of course. Where is she?" As he spoke he was keenly aware that only twenty-four hours earlier he was being asked the same question about Howe's printer's boy. Since then everything seemed to have gone wrong. Jack had escaped from Matt Frygood's clutches. One of Matt's men had drowned in the harbour and the other was at death's door. Matt's black boy (Matt always called him 'boy', though he was nearly forty) had run away and if he felt inclined could take the lid off the entire smuggling operation. But Mr. Hemple felt none of these disasters so keenly as the loss of his daughter.

"Before I answer that question, I want to point out that the last time you saw her I understand that you had hit her hard on the side of her face and were force-marching her into your house. Is that not so?"

"She had run off. It's a parent's right and duty to discipline the child."

"Ah, that may be, but it is the right and duty of all of us to step in when we see cruelty and injustice. Is that not so?"

"I'm not here to talk philosophy with you, Mr. Howe. I have no doubt you'll have every argument at yer damn fingertips. I want me child back, and I want her now."

"Please calm yourself, Mr. Hemple, and sit down. We have some business to complete together." Reluctantly, Mr. Hemple took a seat and stared angrily at Joe, whose smile and good temper was beginning to drive him mad.

"What business?"

"Your daughter, Mr. Hemple, has been terrorized by you. I understand that you have treated her cruelly almost every day, and that is why she was running away from home."

"She's a disobedient little devil…"

" – And that her brother – Harry, is it? – only escapes the same fate by flattering you every moment he can. He is equally terrified of you. – Don't scowl at me, I beg you, Mr. Hemple. These things have been told to my wife by a young girl who I believe loves her father but can no longer endure his brutality. Yes, I know where Lucy is. She is being looked after by Mrs. Howe. But neither she nor I feel like returning her to you unless you are prepared to make a number of commitments to us."

"Commitments?" repeated Mr. Hemple, his eyes rolling.

"Yes, commitments," said Joe, calm as ever. "First, you will never again strike your daughter. Second, you will send away your evil manservant Clifford, and hire a housekeeper who can offer the love and guidance that your daughter needs."

"Are you telling me how to run my household?" Mr. Hemple started to get up, his anger rising.

"No, I am telling you what you must do if you wish to have your daughter back."

"If you don't return her to me instantly I will have you arrested for kidnapping my child."

"And if you do that, I will be publishing a full report of your illegal activities in next week's *Novascotian*."

Mr. Hemple sat bolt upright and stared at his hated enemy.

"What the devil are yer talkin' about? Illegal activities? My firm is a highly respected importin' business. I'm also a magistrate with heavy responsibilities in administerin' the affairs of this town, and – "

"I don't deny any of that, Mr. Hemple. But for some months my staff and I have been looking into your other operations, the ones which are not quite so public or so respectable. Your connection with Matthew Frygood and his cellar, for example…"

Mr. Hemple gave a start.

"Or the voyages of the good ship *Saucy Jane*…or the duty-free rum depot looked after by your man Ezra and that simpleton Silver…Or the baker's cart that runs around town delivering everything but bread…"

"I don't know what you are talking about," muttered Mr. Hemple. He was so shaken that he got up and went to the window to hide his face. He found he was sweating, and pulled out a handkerchief to mop his brow.

"Oh I think you do, Mr. Hemple," replied Joe, "And before very long the whole rotten business will be exposed, and not even your powerful friends will be able to save you from jail, and perhaps the gallows. You're the master-smuggler of Halifax, are you not? Come, come, Josiah, let us not deceive ourselves."

Mr. Hemple turned and faced his accuser.

"You devil!" he said, choking on his words.

"There's one other commitment you must make, Mr. Hemple," continued Joe imperturbably. "For some months you – and also your sad son Harry – have been pursuing a young boy by the name of Jack Dance. You have got it into your heads that because I have befriended him he must be harried and tormented. I must have your word that this will cease, and that from this moment on neither you nor your men will touch a hair of his head."

"I don't even know the boy," muttered Mr. Hemple.

"Oh come on now, my friend! You and your evil crew had him in your grip only yesterday, and I happen to believe that if he hadn't got away you were planning to blackmail me – his life for your good name. Weren't you, Josiah? Come, make a clean breast of it."

Mr. Hemple stared defiantly at Joe Howe. Joe stared calmly back. After almost a minute had passed in utter silence, Mr. Hemple looked away, heaved a huge sigh, and almost crumpled into a chair. Finally he spoke, almost in a whisper:

"And if I make these…these commitments as you call them, you will give me back my daughter?"

"Immediately."

"And you will not do me damage in your newspaper?"

"I give you my word that I will not gather any more information on your activities, and I will not write anything to expose them to the public. But you know as well as I do that this will only delay the matter. I strongly advise you to sever all connection with this wicked traffic you have been living off. Otherwise, even if I do not track you down, others will. And if at any time I receive a written contribution from another source which lays your whole organisation open, I will have no alternative but to publish it. That is what is meant by a free and open press. You magistrates all need to understand the principle – which is why I'm afraid I must bring this amiable talk to an end: I have an urgent appointment with a lawyer. You will guess why." Joe went to the door, opened it, and called out for Mr. McNab. Then he picked up Mr. Hemple's hat and handed it to him. Mr. Hemple pulled himself to his feet, took the hat and managed a grim smile.

"I shall commit myself to these conditions, Mr. Howe. But take care: it may be that before long, it will be you who will be judged the criminal. I will honour my commitments at least until you are in no position to verify them."

"We shall see, won't we," responded Joe pleasantly. "Angus, would you mind accompanying our friend to my home, and telling Mrs. Howe that all is well, and that Mr. Hemple is to be reunited with dear Lucy. They will both know what that means."

❧

The two men left the office and walked down the street. Joe would like to have witnessed the reunion, but he had other fish to fry.

CHAPTER SIXTEEN

FULL HOUSE AT 'THE NOVASCOTIAN'

J ack was itching to get back to work, and walked into the offices of *The Novascotian* the following Monday even earlier than usual, and with a new spring in his step. He and his mother had been thrilled to receive a visit on Sunday afternoon from Mrs. Howe, who had walked up with little Edward to William Alley. While they fussed over her and made tea and scones, Susan Ann told them all that had happened with Lucy and Mr. Hemple, and how Joe had forced the man into an agreement to look after Lucy and never to strike her again.

"Do we really think he'll keep his word?" asked Jack, disbelievingly. He had grown fond of Lucy and couldn't stand to think of her suffering under that mean father of hers.

"Well, Mr. Howe threatened to publish everything he knows about Hemple's smuggling ring unless he honours his commitment. I think he will."

"But if what he is doing is wrong, it *should* be published," said Jack indignantly.

"Now, Jack," said Mrs. Dance, "there you go again, just rushing into things without really knowing anything about it."

"But mother – " began Jack.

"No, he's right, Mrs. Dance – it *should* be exposed for everyone to read and know about. But Mr. Howe felt he had to force Mr. Hemple to treat Lucy properly, and – "

"She hates him," said Jack angrily.

"No, that's not true, dear. She wants to love him. She's never known a mother after all – he's the only parent she has. Mr Howe merely promised that he himself would not write anything in the paper to expose Mr. Hemple. But he made it clear that if he received a contribution from anyone else, he would have to publish it – just as he published George Thompson's letter last month."

"I see," said Jack thoughtfully. "I suppose that's fair."

The talk turned to other things, and Edward and Jack played a game of chess while their mothers chatted about bringing up children, and the continuing cold weather, and Joe Howe's notice of libel and what his options were. Mrs. Dance was no politician, and had little self-confidence, but she read all she could, and she thought things over in a practical and honest way that Mrs. Howe found refreshing. She saw where Jack got some of his perceptions.

"Well, Edward," she said at last, "it's time we left these good friends and walked home. Father will be waiting for us."

They put on their coats and fur hats, and said their goodbyes. Mrs. Dance was proud to have been able to entertain this lovely woman who had been so kind to her, and she hoped she would come again.

"Of course we will, won't we, Edward," smiled Susan Ann.

"Yes, and next time I'll beat Jack at chess!"

Jack wasted no time catching up on the news with Rob and the other apprentices. They were wanting him to tell his story over again, but Mr. McNab shooed them all back into the shop, and Jack started on his rounds in the front office, sweeping and cleaning, changing Mr. Howe's ink – which was always running out, it seemed – and getting the fire going in the big, generous grate.

"Good to have you back, my boy!" boomed Joe from his desk.

"Good to be here, sir!" replied Jack, still on his knees in front of the fire.

"Mrs. Howe told you we have secured a safe passage for you round Halifax?" said Joe, as he settled down for his morning session at the desk.

"Yes, sir. Thank you, sir," replied Jack meekly.

"Don't push your good fortune, all right?"

"Yes, sir – I mean no, sir – I won't."

The office hummed along quietly for a while. Then suddenly things changed. Rob had gone out to pick up some text for a program they were printing, and heard that on Saturday another newspaper, the *Acadian Recorder*, had published a full account of Joe's notice of prosecution. But they had gone further. They invited anyone who had any stories about the way Halifax was administered by the magistrates to go straight to the offices of *The Novascotian* the following Monday and share them with Mr. Howe. Angus dashed off to pick up a copy, and brought it back to show to his chief, who raised his eyes to heaven.

"They might have checked with us," he said mildly.

Within just a few minutes, there was a knocking at the front door. Then another, and another. And another again. Soon the hallway, and Joe's office, and the print-shop, and every other available space in the building, was crammed with excited, jostling citizens. Joe started by trying to take notes as people related their stories, but soon was overwhelmed. He called Angus into his office and told him to take down some of them himself. And still they kept coming. Finally he called for Jack, and passed another batch of the visitors on to him. They were surprised to be telling their tales to a mere lad, but he listened so attentively, wrote so fast, and asked such good questions, that they went away quite satisfied that they had been heard.

By the end of the day, nearly two hundred eager citizens had come with their complaints, their stories of injustice and corruption, their anger and frustration. And Joe Howe had enough material to sink not only the magistrates who ran Halifax, but the entire Governing Council of Nova Scotia.

"I shall want both of you to make me out a full report of everything you've heard," said Joe. "Is that clear?"

Joe was still busy putting his own notes in order when Jack came in with a neat bundle of papers.

"Here you are, sir." He put it on the desk, and Joe picked it up and scanned them quickly.

"Jack, this is very good. Where did you learn to do such a good job of taking down notes?"

"Mrs. Pringle spoke very fast, sir. I got into the habit of it."

Joe smiled. "Good fellow. Thank you very much. This will be most useful."

Joe's visits to his lawyer friends in the previous days had mightily discouraged him. Every one of them had shaken his head just like John Prince, and told him he didn't have a hope of finding a barrister to fight the seditious libel charge. What he had published had certainly brought the magistrates into disrepute, accusing them of criminal acts like taking bribes, using public facilities for personal needs, unequal tax assessments, and everything else. But the fact that all these things were true was apparently no defence in court: if what Joe had printed hurt the reputation of those bumbling magistrates, then he had still committed the crime of seditious libel and must pay the penalty.

Joe's sense of what was right and what was just was deeply offended by the realization that the truth was no defence. His father had brought him up to believe in the power of truth. Was it really possible that the endless stories of neglect, mismanagement and corruption that he and Angus and Jack had heard today were irrelevant?

The lawyers were all sympathetic, though, and had picked dusty books off their shelves to lend them to their good friend Joe Howe. "Maybe *you* can find something in this, Joe," they would say. "But I'll be damned if *I* can." Within a few days he had collected a small library of these heavy, leather-bound volumes, and had lugged them home to his study.

That evening, before the day's work ended, Joe called his staff into the front office.

"My friends," he began, "last time I called you all together, I told you that I was being tried for sedition because I published a letter that told the truth about the town of Halifax. You've seen the hordes of people here today to tell us their stories about how this town is mismanaged. My ears are still ringing from the injustice of it all – I'm sure yours are too, Angus and Jack. But I have to tell you too that I have consulted quite a number of my lawyer friends, and not one of them believes that I have a leg to stand on. There's clearly no point in hiring a lawyer to defend me if none of them think I'm defendable.

"I've talked it over with Mrs. Howe, and I have decided that there is only one course of action open to me. I will take on my *own* defence – without a lawyer."

Jack's eyes opened wide.

"In the next few days I will be spending most of my time in my study at home, reading every single law book I've been given. I'm convinced that there is a way through this, if only I can find it. I shall be in the office early every day until ten, writing my columns for the paper. Then I will be gone. Mr. McNab – Angus – I'm putting a big strain on you, I know that. But we have an important fight on our hands. I know there's not one of you here who would allow the freedom of the press to be swept away by these mediocre and neglectful men.

"Jack, I shall need you to call in at my home after luncheon each day, to see if I need errands to be run, or messages to be sent. Be there sharp at two every afternoon. Is that clear?"

"Yes, sir."

"My faithful apprentices – Rob, Peter, Jim, Bill: I'm going to have to abandon our daily sessions together until after the trial, which looks as though it will take place early in March. Is that understood?"

"That's all right, sir," said Rob, looking around at his fellows. "We'll manage somehow." They all laughed, and Joe laughed with them.

"One more thing," he said. "If I lose the case, which I have to say is entirely possible, I will certainly be fined and may be sent to jail for as long as three years. I'm telling you now, because if this happens it is almost certain that *The Novascotian* will have to be sold, and that you will lose your positions. It is painful for me to have to utter these words, and painful for you to hear them, but there is no point in disguising the fact. I am sure Mrs. Howe will do everything she can to hold our business together, and you know as well as I do how competent she is to do this. But without money we shall be lost. So keep your fingers crossed – and pray a lot!"

The little band of brothers applauded. Joe shook the hands of each one of them in turn. Then he put on his coat and hat, picked up his cane, brandished it in the air with a jolly smile and left for home.

Anyone who knew Angus well would have noticed tears in his eyes. But he barked gruffly at the apprentices to be ready to work all the earlier the next morning, and took his own leave. Jack set out on his twenty-minute walk back to the north end of the town. The lights of the office were doused, and after the apprentices had barred and bolted the doors as usual, they made their way to their spartan sleeping-quarters in the attic above.

CHAPTER SEVENTEEN

JOE HOWE GETS READY TO FIGHT

I n the days that followed, even a complete stranger to the town
of Halifax would have noticed that there was an unusual buzz
of excitement in the streets and the taverns and the coffee-houses
and on the busy wharves. For nearly a hundred years, ever since
the town was founded, its affairs had been directed by a handful
of magistrates who were appointed by the King of England, or by
the governor, who represented the king. So anyone who dared to
challenge these men was immediately accused of rebelling against
the king himself, and could be accused of inciting rebellion. And
since the town was dominated by the frowning Citadel, where
hundreds of the king's soldiers stood forever on guard, there seemed
no hope of ever changing the system.

What was even worse was that the whole of Nova Scotia was
run the same way, by a handful of men hand-picked by the British
government to keep things forever the way they were. Anyone
who suggested that it was time for Nova Scotia to run its own
affairs was seen as a revolutionary. And of course the men in
power looked nervously across the border at the American Union.
Nova Scotia had been the only colony on the Atlantic coast that
had stayed loyal to the English king during the American
Revolution. He could not afford to lose Halifax. And so Halifax
had to be kept on a tight leash.

∽

Now ever since Joe Howe bought *The Novascotian* six or seven
years before, the newspaper had become a place where ordinary

"No, I suppose it depends on what your motive is."

"Exactly. Now, you heard all those stories about the magistrates robbing everyone, didn't you."

"I certainly did. It was terrible."

"So if I destroy the good name of these public robbers by catching them out in their crimes, isn't my motive honourable?"

"Yes, I think it is."

"So should I be punished?"

"No, I don't think you should be. But you told us that the truth was no defence."

"Quite right. But I've found a few passages in these books, by judges and lawyers in Britain, which say that libel should be treated like any other crime."

"What do you mean, sir?"

"I mean that my motive, my intention, should be considered as well as the act of libel itself."

"And if your intention was to do good by printing the letter, then the jury should treat you more kindly because of that?"

"That's the idea — well done!"

"Maybe you can call me or Mr. McNab as witnesses."

"Ah, there you're wrong. In this kind of case, which they call an 'indictment for seditious libel,' I'm not *allowed* to call any witnesses."

"But that's not right!"

"I don't think so either — but of course that's why they chose to do it this way. They're afraid. They don't *want* witnesses. Anyway, enough of that. How are things in the big wide world?"

Jack told Joe the latest stories he had heard, and Joe listened intently. The rumour that he was about to take off for Jamaica made him laugh out loud. "Maybe I should!" he said ruefully. "Things would certainly be quieter."

"Yes, but doesn't Mr. Hemple have all those smuggling friends down there? They would get you the moment you stepped off the ship."

"So you've not forgotten your friend Mr. Hemple?"

"I certainly haven't."

"Watch your step, that's all I say."

"Yes, sir."

Jack did watch his step on his daily wanderings through the town, but he kept his eyes peeled all the same, and took particular note of any suspicious activities. Occasionally he observed the baker's cart jogging through the streets. He often saw Ezra unloading barrels outside Mr. Hemple's warehouse, and once he caught sight of Cliff, clutching his basket and limping through the tangle of small streets that ran behind the market-place smelling eternally of fish. One evening near dusk he saw Matt Frygood being ferried ashore from a ship out in the harbour, the little rowboat almost sinking beneath his tremendous weight. Everything suggested that the smuggling trade was still in full swing, though whether Mr. Hemple was still involved there was no way of knowing.

∞

One day Jack caught sight of his rescuer, Will, selling clothes pins on the street corner. He hadn't seen him since the night of their escape, and ran over to him in delight, pulling eagerly at his sleeve.

"Will!" he cried.

Will started in fright, and jumped away from him. But then he turned and saw who it was.

"Well if it isn't my ol' frien'!– you Jack, right?"

Jack asked how he had been, and heard a woeful tale of Will's adventures. He had twice been nearly re-captured by Frygood's men, but had managed to shake them off both times by being able to out-run them. He had a room with a family on the edge of town, and made a few pennies a day whittling and selling these clothes pins.

Jack led Will to a booth where they could sit and talk, and over a warm drink and a bun he asked Will all sorts of questions about Matt Frygood and his shady friends. Will was too frightened to say much at first, and constantly looked round in case he was being overheard. But before long he was at ease, and between crazy laughs he told Jack a great deal about what used to go on at the cellar, and at the wharf, and in the warehouses. They parted after an hour, and Jack promised to seek him out again.

And every day, Jack took careful note of what he heard and saw, and every day, after supper, he would go up to his little room and write it down.

"What are you writing about all the time?" asked his mother curiously. The schoolboy who had left Mrs. Pringle's before Christmas had become someone else entirely.

"Some day I'm going to be a journalist," said Jack calmly. "I'm practising."

∞

Though Joe Howe had received that letter from the attorney-general in January giving him notice of the magistrates' intention to sue him, he had heard nothing official since, and couldn't help wondering whether they had changed their minds. One day, though, Jack brought him a letter that had arrived at the office late in the day. The letter commanded "Mr. Joseph Howe, printer, of Granville Street, Halifax, to appear at 10 of the clock on the twenty-fourth day of February, in the Year of our Lord Eighteen Hundred and Thirty-Five, before their Lordships the Justices of the Supreme Court of Nova Scotia, to receive formal notice of a bill of indictment to be brought against him." Joe told Jack to take the news back to the office, and called Susan Ann in to show her the letter. She read it twice, and then with tears in her eyes she dropped down on to the sofa beside her husband. Joe put his arm round her and she lay her head against his shoulder, crying quietly.

"Don't cry, my dearest one," said Joe, stroking her hair. "We shall get out of this stronger than ever."

"I hope so," she murmured, wiping her tears.

"I'm sure of it," he said, more to comfort her than because he believed it.

Tuesday, February 24th, came soon enough. The Supreme

Court was housed in the same building as the House of Assembly and the Council Chamber, so it was almost across the street from Joe's house. He had told his wife and his staff at the office not to come, that it was just a formality, but Jack couldn't resist waiting outside Province House to watch his friend walking in. Joe was alone, dressed very smartly in his black morning coat and striped pants, and wearing his long overcoat with the big fur collar, and his best tall hat. He carried his silver-topped cane and nothing else, and Jack, who stood in the shadow of a pillar, thought he looked wonderfully dignified and calm. There were other onlookers around the entrance, and Joe had a smile for them all, turning on the steps to give a cheerful wave before disappearing inside and up the stairs to the court, where the most powerful men in Nova Scotia were assembled – almost all united against him. Jack went straight to the Howes' home to be with Susan Ann, and to wait for news.

Joe's appearance before the court was brief, and he was soon back at home to recount what had happened. He had been indicted on a charge of seditious libel. The indictment had been read by a magistrate who was one of the worst of them all – for years he had been profiting from the supply of the poorhouse with food from his own store and mill, quite against the regulations laid down years before by King George the Third.

Joe was described in the indictment as "a wicked, seditious and ill-disposed person of a most wicked and malicious temper and disposition." Susan Ann cried out in anger, but Jack merely laughed – it was so clearly stupid and untrue. Joe went on to read the rest of the indictment, in which he was accused of "wickedly intending to stir up and excite discontent and sedition among His Majesty's subjects."

"They obviously haven't read *The Novascotian*," commented Jack drily. "You're so loyal to the king and the British Empire that it sometimes almost embarrasses me."

Joe and Susan Ann laughed out loud, but Jack protested:

"It's true, sir. All you have to do is read to them from what you've written in the newspaper, and they'll be shown up as real fools."

"I might just do that, Jack," said Joe. "It's not a bad idea."

They talked a little longer, and then Joe left with Jack for the newspaper offices, to tell his staff that the moment had come: that he was to appear before the Supreme Court on Monday, March 1st, and that the only thing that stood between him and imprisonment and financial ruin was his own skill as a defence lawyer.

"So as you can imagine, I'm in a pickle," he said. "I'm afraid I'm not a lawyer of any kind. And I'm not a public speaker. But I do have some ideas about what I shall say. I shall give it everything I have."

"We are all behind you, Mr. Howe," said Mr McNab heartily, "and what's more we've heard you speak. We all think you'll give them a good run for their money!"

"Thank you Angus. Thank you boys. And now – "

"Back to work!" they all shouted in chorus, and laughed and applauded as they dispersed. Joe laughed with them, then retired to his office to write his leading article for the last issue of his newspaper before the trial. He would have to be very careful. He must not be seen to be stirring up anything at all – simply giving his readers the facts. And this is what he did.

Jack ran all the way home to tell his mother. She went down on her knees, clasped her hands and prayed for Joseph Howe. So did countless other people in the town when they heard the news.

Jack scooted upstairs and wrote many pages into his exercise book. He was worried and nervous – but he was also excited. He felt he was present at the making of history.

CHAPTER EIGHTEEN

MONDAY, MARCH THE FIRST

The first Monday of March was warmer than usual, and the people of Halifax were daring to wonder whether another long winter was just beginning to lose its icy grip on the town. The snowbanks that were piled along the streets and packed down into ice from months of cold were starting to glisten and thaw. Sleighs had been put away for a week or two now, and horses were able to keep their footing on the cobblestones of the main streets and the gravel of the lanes. The sun rose across the harbour, casting a glow of pink over the tops of buildings and lighting up the masts of the jumble of tall ships riding at anchor.

As Jack passed the handsome stone pile of Province House on his way to work, he noticed a crowd of people beginning to gather outside the entrance. Others were hurrying to join them: men and women and even children, coming fast along the street from both directions. He realized they were rushing to stand in line and be sure of a place in the little courtroom when the marshals opened the doors. The other entrance, down on Hollis Street, was even more thickly besieged, and he could hear shouts and cries coming from the excited townsfolk as they jostled and shoved.

When Jack reached the office of *The Novascotian*, he was met in the hall by Mr. McNab, who was dressed as though for a funeral, all in black. Behind him stood Peter and Bill and Jim and Rob, all got up in their Sunday clothes and like Mr. McNab looking a lot smarter than usual.

"There y'are, Jack," he said. "Now listen to me: I've told the boys that Mr. Howe's closing the office until the trial's over. He's given me passes into the courtroom for all of us. Take one of these. It may be the last thing ye ever get from him," he added mournfully, handing each of them a ticket.

"There's a lot of people there, already, Mr. McNab," said Jack. "Maybe we should go down right away."

"Took the words straight out of my mouth as usual, Mr. Smart Alec," replied Mr. McNab. "Off ye go, and I'll be locking up behind ye."

An hour later there was a mass of several hundred people crowded around each great door of Province House. The sun was up and the mood was merry. The doors had opened for the judges and the judge's clerks, and then from time to time for the Halifax magistrates, most of whom were greeted with muttered insults and even boos, as they stalked up the steps trying to maintain their dignity. Jack enjoyed watching one of them dodge a rotten apple as he stepped inside. He looked for Mr. Hemple, but in vain.

Soon after, the doors were officially opened, and those with passes were let in. Jack and the apprentices had by this time wormed their way to the front of the crowd, bringing a reluctant Mr. McNab along with them, so they were almost the first inside. The lads ran up the stairs and grabbed the seats in the front row of the little gallery. Mr. McNab followed at a more dignified pace, but was happy to take the seat they had kept for him.

From here they could get the best view of everything that went on down below on the floor of the courtroom. On the far wall, panelled in wood, hung the royal coat of arms, and below it stood the high bench where the judges would sit. Mr. McNab pointed out the dock where the accused would have to stand, and the tables to right and left below the judges where the crown attorneys would take their places.

The town magistrates and other local bigwigs were already sitting down in the front of the audience area, dressed in their fine coats and hats, and laughing and chatting as though they were waiting for a game to start. Jack saw one of them taking snuff and promptly having fifty sneezes. Another took a silver flask out of his pocket, and treated himself to a generous sip of something or other before offering it to his neighbours. He watched each new arrival as they all took their seats, waving to their friends and chattering gaily. He recognized many of them as Joe Howe's friends, and was especially happy to see Mrs. Howe entering with Edward beside her, and taking their seats near the front.

To his left he could look out of the tall, graceful windows and watch the crowd in Hollis Street growing and growing. Soon the whole street was packed to the far side, and traffic of horses and carts and the occasional carriage had a hard time making its way through. There were shouts and whistles and catcalls – the excitement both in the room and outside was electric, and Jack found himself so keyed up he could hardly stay in his seat. It was the first time he had even been inside a court of law, and everything was new and fascinating.

In a very short time the whole courtroom was jammed, with people standing at the sides of the floor below, and craning forward from the back of the gallery, behind Jack and his friends. Jack recognized all sorts of people among them. Mr. George Thompson, who was in the gallery close by, nodded at Jack when he spotted him. He saw Cliff standing at the side down below, scowling as usual and looking like some kind of evil bird. Even Matt Frygood was there, taking up two chairs with his enormous size, and smoking a long clay pipe as he joked noisily with the men around him. The magistrates were mostly sitting together, but there was no sign of Mr. Hemple all through the day.

In came the twelve jury members, taking their seats on the right, and looking very solemn and even nervous. Jack thought they all seemed very old, and hoped that was a good thing. He was glad to see Mr. Lawson among the jury; at least one of them was a friend of Joe Howe's.

In came the lawyers for the Crown in their black robes and white collars. They set out their papers on the table in front of them and took their seats, talking earnestly with their heads close together.

Soon after, Joseph Howe made his entrance, and the buzz of excitement among the onlookers rose even higher. Formally dressed in his black frock coat and black trousers, he was carrying a briefcase in one hand and his old carpet-bag in the other. He looked immediately for his wife and smiled at her, then strode to the defence table. He brought out a mass of notes and documents, and laid them out carefully. Then he opened the carpet-bag and fished out a pile of big books with markers in them. He organised them on his table and took his seat. But the constable of the court went over to him and spoke a word in his ear, at which Joe Howe got up again and walked beside the constable to the prisoner's dock, where he stood facing the court. He looked very calm, Jack thought, and very dignified.

Finally, the Clerk of the Court, dressed in a strange black costume with breeches and silver buckled shoes, entered from a door at the back and called out: "Silence in court! All stand!" He had to repeat himself a couple of times before everyone stood and the room was quiet.

In came the three judges in their billowing black gowns. They climbed the steps to their long bench and sat facing the room. Everyone sat down again, and the Clerk of the Court had to call out again: "Silence! Order in court!" At last there was complete quiet. The trial of Joseph Howe was ready to begin.

When Jack talked afterwards about that momentous day, he could never quite decide what the high point of it had been for him. Was it the moment when, after the prosecution had gone over the libel charges, the judges called for the defence, and Mr. Howe bowed and walked calmly across the room from the prisoner's dock to his place at the defence table, and began to speak? Was it when he mentioned poor Miss Hogg and the money she was still owed by the magistrates — a story that Jack had given him? Was it the moment when Jack realized fully the strategy Joe was using: not trying to deny the libel but instead explaining the motive for his "crime" by describing all the terrible things the magistrates had been doing? Was it when the crowd roared with laughter at Joe's picture of the way the prison was run, with prisoners running around doing chores for the man in charge, even making boots and shoes for his family and a birdcage for his daughter? Was it when he put down his papers and went over to the jury to beg them to do their duty and acquit him, making a passionate plea for Nova Scotia to have a free and "unshackled" press? Was it when he mentioned his wife and his children and the "orphan apprentices in his office," none of whom would ever allow the press to be wounded through him? "We would wear the coarsest raiment," he said. "We would eat the poorest food, and crawl at night into the veriest hovel in the land to rest our weary limbs, but with cheerful and undaunted hearts; and these jobbing justices would feel that one frugal, united family had withstood their persecution, defied their power, and maintained the freedom of the press." Rob turned to his fellow apprentices and they wanted to cheer, but Mr. McNab hushed them.

Joe Howe spoke for hours, and there were times when the young boys – and even Jack – almost found themselves nodding off. But not for long: his voice was so strong and warm, he smiled so confidently and made the audience laugh and cry with so much ease, that they found themselves not wanting to miss a moment. Again and again the judges had to call for order in court – there was so much laughing and cheering and applause that Jack felt the whole town would explode if Joe was found guilty. But then these judges and the whole system that they stood for were so powerful that they might pay no attention to what the people wanted. It was all up to the jury, Jack realized, and he kept looking over at their faces, trying to guess what they were thinking. Once he saw a white-haired gentleman among them crying a little as Joe described the way the poor were being treated. He hoped the others felt the same way.

The sun moved slowly out of sight round the building, but still

Joe spoke. Outside, those of the crowd not able to get in still stood. Occasionally someone came out from the court to tell them what was happening. It began to get dark, and still Joe talked on. Finally he told the jury that the freedom of the press was in their hands, and that they must do their duty and defend it by letting him go.

When Joe sat down, there was spontaneous applause from the crowd, which the judges stopped very quickly and harshly. They directed Joe back into the prisoner's dock – he walked there calm as ever – and said they wanted to adjourn the court for the day and start again tomorrow. One of Mr. Howe's lawyer friends stood up and protested, saying that this would not be fair to Mr. Howe, because his arguments would no longer be fresh in the jurors' minds the next day. But the judges had their way. The court was closed until ten the following morning. Everyone stood while the three judges walked out, and then the whole room broke into excited chatter and shouts and laughter as they stood up and stretched their legs after the long, long day, and made their way to the doors.

Many of Joe's friends came up to him and shook his hand, but he didn't talk with them long – he was plainly worn out. Jack ran down from the gallery into the courtroom and helped him put the books back into his bag.

"Well done, sir," he whispered. "It was wonderful."

"We'll see," said Joe shortly, with a faint smile. Susan Ann came over and embraced him, and the little family group took off home, with Jack heading out towards the North End at a run, eager to tell his mother of the day's events. The crowd inside and outside dispersed, and soon the whole courtroom lay empty and dark, as though resting quietly before the decision of the following day – "the most important," as Joe had said at the end of his speech, "ever delivered before the Supreme Court of Nova Scotia."

CHAPTER NINETEEN

THE VERDICT

I t was still early next morning, and dark as pitch, when Jack bounded out of bed. He ran downstairs, as he did every winter morning, to get the woodstove started again for his mother – then carried a taper back up to his room to light his candle. This time, though, when he had finished dressing, he bent down, groped under his bed and slowly brought out a large brown envelope. From it he drew a dozen sheets of lined buff-coloured paper, held together by a big brass clip and covered on both sides with his own writing—surprisingly fluid and well-formed for a child of his age. Sitting on the bed, he began for the twentieth time to read, occasionally stopping to make a correction. When he reached the end, he thought for a moment.

"What are you doing, dear?" called his mother from across the hall.

"We don't have to be at the office before Mr. Howe's trial starts again. I'm just looking at something."

"Well, come on down now and have your breakfast."

"Yes, Mother."

Taking a deep breath, he folded the sheets once again and stuffed them back into the envelope.

"What's that, Jack?" asked his mother, motioning with her teacup towards the envelope that Jack had set on the table beside him while he ate his porridge.

"It's some writing I've been doing," said Jack, rather mysteriously.

"For Mr. Howe?" asked Mrs. Dance.

"Yes." Jack wouldn't be drawn any further. As he started to put on his coat and boots, his mother became more and more puzzled.

"Jack, you don't have to leave yet! The trial doesn't start again till ten, you told me."

"Yes, I know, but I have to see someone first, down at the market."

"Oh no – no, Jack! You're not getting caught up in all that smuggling nonsense again are you? I won't have it – you've already made me sick with worry with all your goings on. If this work at the newspaper is so dangerous I'm going to have you taken out of that office right away. There's all sorts of other work to be had. You simply don't care about…" And Mrs. Dance burst into tears. Jack got up, ran over and put his arm around his mother.

"Don't worry, Mother," he said. "I promise I won't do anything to get me into trouble. I promised Mr. Howe the same thing."

"You're all I have, Jack."

"I know, Mother. But I made a promise to myself too," Jack went on: "You know about Mr. Hemple and all his smuggling friends, and everything that's going on down there on the wharves."

"I know far more about Hemple than I want to – he's the man who nearly killed my boy." She started to sob again.

"Don't cry, Mother." He paused and stroked her greying hair. "Mother, Mr. Howe told Mr. Hemple that he wouldn't write anything in the newspaper about him if he made some commitments."

"Yes, like promising not to harm my boy."

"Yes, and looking after Lucy properly – and getting rid of his servant Cliff – and closing down his smuggling business."

"Who knows whether he has been keeping his word? I don't trust him an inch."

"No, nor do I," said Jack, his grey eyes looking steadily in front of him, his arm still round his mother's neck. "So I have been doing some scouting around these last few weeks. I've talked a lot to Will, the man who rescued me. And he's led me to some other people that know a lot about the smuggling ring. And I've met Lucy again secretly. So I've discovered a lot of things."

"And are you trying to tell me that you haven't been in danger doing all this?" Mrs. Dance looked at him and shook her head. "I think you'll never learn."

"Mother, Mr. Howe always tells us that we must stand up for what is right, and that sometimes this means taking some risks. But I'm very careful, I swear. And instead of getting caught having adventures, I'm just watching and listening – and writing everything down." He got up and picked his envelope up off the table. "This is it."

"What are you going to do with that? If they caught you with it you would – "

"They won't catch me with it," Jack broke in firmly. "If Mr. Howe loses his case, and goes to prison, I'll have to hide it somewhere or even burn it. But if he does lose, there'll be a lot of much more terrible things happening. No one will worry about me."

"And if he wins?"

"I'm going to put it straight into his hands to publish in *The Novascotian*. He'll probably have to re-write it a bit, but…"

"I'm sure he will. You're just a baby – you can't write for a newspaper, you silly boy!"

"Maybe not. But I'm trying. It's what I want to do, Mother. I've told you that before."

"Anyway, Mr. Howe promised Mr. Hemple he wouldn't expose him in the paper."

"He said he wouldn't do it himself. But if someone else sent in an article, he said he would have to publish it. So here it is." Mrs. Dance looked at this boy of hers, so young, so bright, so determined, and finally smiled and kissed him.

"Bless you, Jack. Off you go now, and I'll be praying for Mr. Howe all day. Mind you tell me the news as soon as you can."

"Yes, Mother." He gave her a quick kiss in return, then got swiftly into his boots, threw on his jacket and cap, stuffed the brown envelope into his satchel and was out of the door. "By-ee!" As he skipped down the street the sun was coming up on another clear day, and at the corner he thought he heard a robin sing. Yes, spring was in the air.

News had got round the town that Joe Howe's trial had not finished the previous day, and the crowd at Province House the next morning was even thicker than before. Everyone was talking with wonder and disbelief about the way that Joe had defended himself by bringing up all the corruption, incompetence and stupidity of the magistrates and their system. There was tremendous joy at his courage and daring, but there was also a great deal of fear about his fate. The magistrates had the council behind them, and the governor—even the king. Was there any way that these powerful authorities could be challenged?

By ten o'clock the courtroom was packed once again. The crown attorneys were crouched solemnly at their tables, Joe Howe was sitting solemnly in the prisoner's dock, the jury were sitting solemnly in their places, and the judges were sitting solemnly on their bench – like faces on a deck of cards, Jack thought to himself.

The chief justice began to speak. His job was to sum up the arguments on each side of the case, and then give instructions to the jury. He spoke in a thin, piping voice, and he hadn't got very far before it was clear whose side he was on. He said there was no doubt that seditious libel had been committed by the accused, and that the jury's duty was to find him guilty. Angus McNab moaned under his breath, and the apprentices' hearts sank, as they realized what was being said. Jack was not sad, he was angry, and felt like standing up and telling the judge he was a fool. He looked over at the jury. He couldn't tell what they were thinking – they just looked back at the judge without any expression on their faces.

Finally, the jury were instructed to leave and not to return until they had reached a unanimous decision. They left the courtroom by a side door, with all eyes upon them, and the judges filed out again behind the clerk of the court. Joe was taken by a constable through another door, and as soon as he was gone the room broke out into excited chatter, as people got up and strolled about and talked to their friends. Loud laughter came from among the magistrates, and Jack saw Cliff limping over to Matt Frygood and talking in his ear. They might be in for a long wait – Mr. McNab told the boys that juries could take hours and even days to reach a verdict of "guilty" or "not guilty."

"They all have to agree, that's the problem," he said, as pessimistic as ever: "I hope you lads have all been lookin' for jobs somewhere else. There's no doubt Mr. Howe's going to be put away. No more *Novascotian*, that's for sure."

"Don't say that," piped up Jack. "Just say 'we'll see.'"

"We'll see," repeated Mr. McNab sarcastically, shaking his head.

At that very moment the door at the back opened again. The Clerk of the Court called for everyone to stand, and then led the judges back to their bench. Joe Howe returned to the room, and was led to the prisoner's dock. The people hurried back to their seats, and a sudden hush fell on the room. Then the side door opened again, and the members of the jury filed in and took their seats.

∞

The chief justice turned to the foreman of the jury, who was standing.

"So, Foreman, have you reached a verdict?"

"We have, M'Lord," said the foreman, strongly, and looking him in the eye.

"And what is your verdict?"

There was a pause. The foreman looked around at his fellow jurors, and then back at the judges. Finally he spoke:

"Not guilty, Your Lordship."

There was a moment of silence, then the courtroom broke out in applause and shouts of bravo and laughter and even weeping. Jack couldn't believe his ears, and gave Mr. McNab, who had promptly burst into tears, a mischievous dig in the ribs.

"You see, sir! You see!" He chattered happily with Rob and the other apprentices, and looked down again at the scene below. The judges had filed out, and he was just in time to see Matt Frygood, with great alarm on his face, puffing and wheezing as he moved his great bulk hurriedly between the chairs and out of the door. He saw a little knot of magistrates arguing angrily amongst themselves, then dispersing and walking out not looking to right or left, with people shouting after them as they went. Cliff had disappeared, and Joe Howe himself was scarcely visible – there were so many friends and admirers crowded round him, embracing him and almost shaking his hand off. As soon as news of the verdict got out to the waiting crowd outside, a huge cheer went up, and people started breaking into song; Jack saw them actually starting to dance in the street. It was a wonderful moment. Thanks to Joe Howe – and thanks to that brave jury that had refused to follow the judge's advice – the people of Nova Scotia were a big step closer to having charge of their own affairs. Everyone knew it, and everyone – except of course the magistrates and their powerful friends – rejoiced.

∞

Mr. McNab had pulled himself together, and was now giving instructions to the apprentices, who were told dourly that they must be reporting for work in just a few minutes at the office of *The Novascotian*. "To work again!" cried Rob with a laugh.

Jack took advantage of their little meeting to pick up his satchel and make his way through the crowd on the staircase as they came down from the gallery. Being small he was able to dodge around and below people, and was soon in the main hall. As he got there, Joe was being swept out through the main doors of the courtroom. A bunch of men were taking hold of him and lifting him onto their shoulders with shouts of laughter and applause, and they started carrying him across the hall and down the stairs to the exit doors, followed by a mass of people. He was smiling and waving to everyone around, just managing to hold on to his hat and his cane. He spotted Jack and gave him a wink as he went by – to Jack's delight.

As the procession went through the doors a mighty shout went up from the crowd still gathered outside. Then the whole caval-cade, with the burly figure of Joe bobbing awkwardly above the crowd, moved slowly up the street to his home, and finally deposited him at his front door. While he stood there waving at the crowd and thanking them for their support, someone cried out "Three cheers for Joe!" and the cheers echoed and re-echoed down the street and into the hearts of the people.

✎

Jack, his own heart full of pride and happiness, was watching all this from the edge of the crowd, when suddenly he felt his satchel being pulled violently from off his shoulder. He jumped round and grabbed hold of it, wrenching it away from his attacker. Then he heard a cackling laugh and looked up to see who had tried to rob him. It was Cliff.

"Something important in your satchel, Mr. Dance?" said Cliff with his usual unhappy scowl, but cackling at the same time.

"Oh, Cliff, you really scared me," said Jack.

"That was my idea," said Cliff. "Well, you got what you want-ed. Mr. Howe's a free man."

"Yes. And you promised me that if he was found not guilty you would help me." Jack looked up at him with those searching, hon-est grey eyes of his.

"I did. And here I am. Come with me. We need to hurry."

CHAPTER TWENTY

SMUGGLERS AWAY

Anyone who knew Jack, and knew of his adventures over the last few months, would have been horrified to see him trotting down the street beside the limping, crow-like figure of Cliff, and would have immediately called for help and raced to his rescue. But every single friend of Joe's, except Jack himself, was crowding outside and inside the home of the Howes. Susan Ann had quickly sent out for food and wine and cider, and the living-room was packed with excited and joyous people.

Cliff led Jack swiftly down the steep streets that led to the wharves. As they approached the offices of "Josiah Hemple, Merchant," he laid his hand on Jack's arm and said, "This way."

He dived off into a little side alley behind some shacks, and after many twists and turns came to the small door of a shed. He knocked three times on the door. After a few seconds they heard bolts being drawn back, and the door opened slowly. It was Will! Jack greeted him with a hearty handshake, but Will put his finger to his lips and beckoned them in. Jack hesitated, but gathered up his courage and walked into the shadowy shed. As his eyes got used to the dark he could see Will and Cliff creeping up to a small window at the far end. "Come here," whispered Cliff to Jack in his gravelly voice. "We should be just in time." Jack groped his way to the dusty window, and looked out.

What a sight met his eyes! Tied up at the wharf lay a large schooner, its black and gold paint shining in the sun. Its gangways were down, and backward and forward, up and down the narrow boards tramped, scores of dockworkers, bowed over under heavy loads as they toiled up to the ship, then ran back down for another load. On the deck, sailors were packing the goods onto pallets, and another sailor was winching them into the ship's hold. By the deckhouse stood the captain and first mate. Jack's eyes moved to the stern of the ship where he saw, written in gold letters:

SAUCY JANE
Yarmouth, Nova Scotia

Striding around on the wharf beside the dockworkers stood Matt Frygood, huge in his blue greatcoat, swearing and shouting. He had a horsewhip in his hand, which again and again he cracked on the paving stones to get the workers to move faster. Every few minutes a fresh horse and wagon arrived from the street with more packages. The goods had obviously been packed in a hurried and careless way, and Jack thought he recognized some of the strange objects he had seen in the smugglers' cellar, sticking crazily out of boxes and crates.

It didn't take long, in fact, for Jack to realize that there was a massive removal operation going on. Will laughed quietly behind him as they all watched. "They're gettin' out!" he said: "They're runnin' away!" And he chortled away until Cliff motioned to him to be quiet – their hiding-place was so close that the men passing by could easily have seen and heard them.

Within a few minutes, as they watched, there was a new commotion on the wharf. A smart carriage and pair drew up at the edge of the street, and out of the carriage stepped—yes, it was…none other than His Worship, Josiah Hemple, Esquire. Out of the carriage behind him jumped his bulky son Harry and then, more slowly, little Lucy. They were both dressed in travelling clothes, and carried small cases. Behind the carriage, another vehicle pulled up, and Jack recognized the baker's van that had carried him away a few weeks earlier. Ezra and Silver jumped off the driver's box and opened the back doors. They began heaving everything out of the van and piling it onto the wharf: clocks and carpets and chairs, and oil-paintings and boxes of silver, and chests and trunks.

Mr. Hemple strode over to a couple of the dockworkers as they came off the boat and directed them to leave what they were doing and pick up his baggage and furniture. They were starting towards the pile when Matt Frygood barred their way and sent them back. Mr. Hemple ran up to Matt, and there in the middle of the wharf they had an almighty shouting match, with Matt cracking his whip and threatening Mr. Hemple, who had to jump out of the way to escape it. Then Matt staggered over to Mr. Hemple's goods and began kicking them and pushing them until they lay all over the ground. Mr. Hemple was beside himself with rage. He reached inside his coat and pulled out a long, evil-looking pistol.

All this time Harry and Lucy had been cowering in the distance, but now Lucy jumped up and ran straight towards Mr. Hemple:

"Father! Don't!" She grabbed his arm, but he shook her off with an oath, took aim at Matt Frygood and fired. The ball hit Frygood in the shoulder. He howled with pain and staggered back. Lucy let out a scream of horror and ran off down the wharf and out of sight.

At that moment a pair of silver-grey horses galloped along Water Street, pulling a large conveyance. They stopped at the wharf with a clatter of hooves, and out jumped half a dozen constables, a sheriff and two soldiers in uniform, carrying muskets at the ready.

Mr. Hemple was about to fire a second shot at the writhing Matt Frygood when he caught sight of the constables and soldiers in the distance. With a cry, he turned and raced towards the *Saucy Jane*, pushing one of the dockworkers right into the water as he barged past him on the gangway. He took no notice, but shouted to the captain on the foredeck:

"Cast off, yer fool! Get the hell out of here!" He turned back to the shore. "Harry! Lucy! Get on board for Pete's sake!"

Harry scrambled out from behind some crates and scampered in terror up one of the gangways just before it fell off the edge of

the wharf and slid into the water. "Lucy!" shouted Mr. Hemple again. "Lucy!" But Lucy was nowhere to be seen.

Before Mr. Hemple had shouted at him, Captain Watts had already seen the constables arriving, and had been barking orders to his sailors on the deck. One of them jumped onto the wharf at the bow of the ship and slipped the heavy rope off its bollard. The one controlling the winch jumped to the gunwale and picked up a pole to move the boat away from the wharf, leaving the winch chain to unravel with a loud clatter and drop its cargo with a sickening crash into the hold. The dockworkers threw down their loads and scattered all over the wharf.

The constables seemed taken aback by the scene in front of them, and it took time for them to work out what was happening. Mr. Hemple's high-strung horses had taken fright and were dragging his carriage with them as they cantered away up the street. The constables ran first to Matt Frygood, who by this time was sprawling on the ground screaming and clutching his shoulder, which was oozing blood. Ezra and Silver started running away, and two constables went loping after them. One of the soldiers fired his musket at no one in particular, and the other took up a kneeling position behind a barrel, looking very business-like but in fact keeping well out of the way of any further shots.

By the time the sheriff had taken in all the activity around the ship, it was moving away from the wharf. The captain was giving orders for the mainsail to be raised and it inched up, catching the wind as it went and gradually moving the vessel faster out into the harbour. When the constables arrived at the edge of the wharf, the boat was well away and gathering speed. There was nothing they could do. Mr. Hemple had escaped.

The trio in the shed watched this amazing scene with a mixture of astonishment, awe and laughter. But while the excitement was still dying down, Jack turned and started running toward the door.

"Now where you be goin', Jack?" asked Will coming towards him.

"Lucy," said Jack. "I'm going to find Lucy."

<hr>

It was nearly two hours later that a small and motley group, led by Jack, arrived on the doorstep of Joe Howe's home. People were still standing in the street, chatting. A small brass band had arrived and was serenading Joe with cheerful tunes from the sidewalk. The crowd was singing along, and it felt like a public holiday. Jack was welcomed warmly at the door by Betty, who had been run off her feet since the end of the trial and was now ready to drop.

"Why, there you are, Jack!" she panted, wiping her hands on her apron. "Your mother's here – go and see her – she's worried sick for you. Who are these people?" She looked suspiciously at the group Jack was bringing in.

"This is Will, who saved my life," said Jack. "This is Cliff, who was once my enemy but is now my friend. And this – " he went round behind Cliff and dragged her out, " is my good friend Lucy."

"Well, come along in," sighed Betty.

Cliff didn't feel comfortable going into the house, and followed Betty into the kitchen, taking a grateful Will with him. Jack protested, but Cliff was determined – it was only a few weeks ago that Joe Howe had been the hated target of Mr. Hemple and his men, and he was keen to put off an encounter with the day's hero. Jack took Lucy by the hand and led her into the crowded living-room. Mrs. Dance caught sight of him immediately and broke off her chat with a group of other women as he ran towards her.

"Hello, Mother!" he said happily, giving her a fond hug: "How wonderful you're here! Did you walk all the way into town?"

"I couldn't wait any longer to hear the news. They've been so kind. And this is Lucy, isn't it? I remember you."

"Lucy's very brave," said Jack, "and I've asked her to stay with us. Is that all right?"

"We'll see," said Mrs. Dance, surprised by the news but so happy to see Jack that nothing else seemed to matter. At that moment Mrs. Howe came into the room with a brimming pitcher of cider.

When she saw Jack and Lucy, she put it down and kissed them both.

"Isn't this the greatest day, Jack!" she exclaimed. "I still can't believe it."

"The best day ever," replied Jack, his eyes shining. "And you don't know it all yet! Where's Mr. Howe?"

"He went up to his room. Poor fellow, he's been under terrible strain for weeks, and he's never shown it until now. He's completely exhausted."

"I have something for him. And I've got some news he should have right away."

"Oh, go upstairs — I don't expect he'll mind seeing his troublesome printer's devil. Lucy, you stay here with us."

Jack scampered up the big wide staircase he knew so well, and knocked at Joe Howe's bedroom door.

"Who is it?"

"It's Jack, sir. I have something for you."

"I'll be with you in a moment." Jack opened his satchel and pulled out the big brown envelope that he had been carrying around since dawn. He waited a minute or two, then the door opened and Joe appeared. He had taken off his collar and cravat, and was standing in his shirtsleeves, his suspenders looped around below his waist. Jack looked up at his hero's strong, generous face — and saw with amazement that Joe had been crying. There were tears in his eyes and drops running down his cheeks. He was holding a handkerchief and wiping the tears away.

"Are you all right, sir?" asked Jack in alarm.

"Yes. Yes, I'm all right, Jack."

"I didn't know…" Jack paused. "I didn't know grown up men cried tears. I thought it was only women who did that."

"Don't you believe it, Jack. Don't you believe it." He looked down at the boy with a tired smile. "So what do you have for me?"

"This, sir." He handed him the envelope, which Joe took with a little frown.

"What is it?"

"It's an article for *The Novascotian*."

"Why, thank you! Who does it come from?"

"From me, sir."

"You wrote it?"

"Yes, sir."

"Well I'm blessed!"

"I've been working on it for weeks, sir. If you hadn't won today I would probably have burnt it. And I've more news since that was written, sir. Can I tell it to you?"

"Go on downstairs, dear Jack, and wait for me there. When the crowd's gone home we can sit around the fire and you can tell us all your story."

"All right, sir." Jack turned to go.

"Oh, and Jack…"

"Yes, sir?"

"I know you want to be a writer and a journalist…"

"Yes, very much, sir."

"But you know, the best way to start is by working in a printshop, just as I did."

"Oh I know, sir."

"That way, you really get to know how words work and how to use them."

"Yes, sir."

"So Jack…"

"Yes, sir?"

"You've done enough devilling for me. I want you to start next Monday as an apprentice. Would you like that?"

Jack looked at him, and could hardly get the words out. "V –v- very much, sir."

"You'll be the youngest apprentice I ever had – but you may turn out to be the cleverest! Now run along and I'll see you downstairs." Jack started down the corridor to the landing.

"And thank you for everything, Jack."

"That's all right, sir," said Jack lightly. He flew down the stairs three at a time.

The sun had been gently thawing the winter ice all day, and had now set in a blaze of scarlet over Citadel Hill. But the old streets were still alive with people. The happy outcome of Joe's trial had set off a kind of spring carnival, and there was singing and shouting and games, music, and all kinds of fun. Somebody had set a bonfire out of old fruit crates in the middle of the market-place, and it was blazing merrily, with ragged children standing round it holding out their hands. The people of Halifax had more hope in their hearts than they'd had for many a year.

The Howes' closest friends had finally said their goodbyes to Susan Ann and left, and she had gone upstairs to bring Joe down. With her last ounce of energy, and grumbling a little of course, Betty had set still more bread and jam and cold meats and cakes on the table by the fire, and Jack had finally coaxed Cliff and Will out of the kitchen to join the family circle. Will sat cross-legged on the floor and gazed into the fire. It was the first time he had been warm all winter. Cliff looked moodily into space, thinking sadly of his past life and wondering what would be his future. Several times Lucy had been on the edge of tears, and Jack had his arm around her. Mrs. Dance sat in the armchair closest to the fire, and leaned back with her eyes closed. For her it felt like that wonderful Christmas all over again.

The door opened, and in came Susan Ann and Joe, arm in arm. Joe held Jack's closely written sheets in his hand.

"Well, Jack, you've amazed me again: this is not at all a bad piece of work, and Mrs. Howe agrees with me. How on earth did you find all that out about our town's most successful smugglers? I don't think I could print it straight into the paper — we would need to fix a few things — but it's a great start." He sat down in his big chair, and Susan Ann brought him some cake and cider.

"I couldn't have done it without these people here," said Jack modestly, but glowing inside at the compliment. "It's been specially hard for Lucy, but she couldn't go on being a prisoner, could she? That's when Cliff — this is Cliff by the way — took pity on her, and came to me to let me know." He picked up some toast and started buttering it for her.

"So your father didn't get a housekeeper to look after you, Lucy?"

"No, he never did," said Lucy in a faint voice.

"Does he know you're here now?"

Jack butted in. "Sir, have you heard what happened down on the wharf today?"

"I've heard nothing."

So Jack found himself – not for the first time in his young life – telling a story to a crowd of people. He described the whole amazing scene on the wharf: Matt Frygood and his whip, the loading up of the contraband, Mr. Hemple's arrival with Harry and Lucy, the wounding of Matt Frygood, his capture by the bumbling police and soldiers, and the hurried departure of *Saucy Jane*. Lucy cried several times, but refused to leave the room. Will and Cliff occasionally put in a word, but it was Jack's moment, and he enthralled them all.

"What I still don't understand," said Joe when he had listened to the end, "is what made them decide to leave just at this moment. Why were they in such a tearing hurry?"

"I think Jack has to take some of the credit for that," said Cliff from his corner, and everyone turned round in surprise – including Jack himself.

"How do you mean?" asked Jack.

"Jack told me a few days ago about the news story he was writing. Before I left Mr. Hemple for the last time, I told him that there would be an article in print in Mr. Howe's paper this week if Mr. Howe won his case, and that it would reveal everything about Mr. Hemple and his activities – including the treatment of his children."

"I can't believe it! Is that why he wasn't at the trial with all the other magistrates?" asked Susan Ann.

"Yes, ma'am. He was burning his papers, and drinking a lot, and getting ready for a quick flight – Silver was told to run and give him the verdict the moment it came out. Matt made preparations to run away too, but he was convinced you would lose, Mr. Howe – in fact he had a big wager on it with one of the officers at the Citadel. So he sat in the courtroom until the last moment, and rushed out to get away before having to pay it."

"Where is he now?"

"I was talking to someone outside who said he was in the hospital room at Bridewell Jail, and that he's expected to live."

"Sounds like another trial ahead of us," said Joe with a smile.

"What about the police?" asked Mrs. Dance. "I thought they only did what the magistrates told them to do."

"I can claim some credit for that, I think," said Cliff. "I went to the town office this morning and told them that Mr. Hemple's business was going to be attacked, and that he had sent me to ask for their protection."

"So that's why they looked so confused!" cried Jack.

"Of course! They came to defend one of their masters, and found he was out on the wharf shooting his friends and running away from the law."

"They didn' know what to do, they thought they was goin' crazy!" said Will.

There was a knock at the door, and soon Angus McNab and all of Joe's four apprentices filed in awkwardly and found seats wherever they could. Joe had sent for them to come and join the celebrations at the end of the working day, and he made a gracious little speech to thank them for their loyalty during the long ordeal of the libel case. Angus brought happy news as well: someone had dropped into the newspaper office to say that following the trial the magistrates of Halifax had all resigned. There was a cheer from the whole company. They all knew that it was Joe Howe, and Joe Howe alone, who had "brought down the mighty from their seats," – as Angus said.

The talk around the fire went on long into the evening, with Joe Howe in his element, surrounded by family and colleagues and friends, and no one wanting to let go of this wonderful day. He told stories and made them laugh. He talked politics. He discussed the smuggling problem. He talked about Nova Scotia

and all the splendid things that could happen in this little country if people would only believe in it. He talked about young people and how important it was that they had a chance to go to school and learn about life and science and the arts. He talked of the plight of black people and the native people in the province, and the need to give them the full rights of citizens. He talked about his love of books. He talked about the new steamboats, and the new railways, and all the opportunities for trade and commerce that these new inventions could open up. All these were serious subjects, but somehow he made them all sound so interesting that everyone listened and thought along with him – even the youngest. Jack was entranced.

And while Joe talked, and his fire crackled, fires all over Halifax were crackling too, while around them sat hundreds of other families and their friends, talking excitedly of their hero Joe Howe and what he had done for them and for the town that momentous day. It was another story, of course, in the homes of the powerful folk who had grown rich for years by feeding off the little town of Halifax and the little province of Nova Scotia. Here there was anger and there was fear. And in Government House, over his long dinner table of shining mahogany, the governor discussed the situation gloomily with his advisers.

Spring was finally in the air, ice packs were melting along the rivers and in the creeks, and everyone could sense that at last, in this little corner of the world, change was on the way.